SERENITY
FOR
ST. PATRICK'S DAY

Children of The Others Collection -
Book Three

SERENITY FOR ST. PATRICK'S DAY

Children of The Others Collection - Book Three

A. Dragonblood

Illustrated by Ted Kay

authorHOUSE®

AuthorHouse™
1663 Liberty Drive
Bloomington, IN 47403
www.authorhouse.com
Phone: 1-800-839-8640

First published by AuthorHouse 8/23/2011

ISBN: 978-1-4634-4120-3 (e)
ISBN: 978-1-4634-4121-0 (sc)

Library of Congress Control Number: 2011913692

Printed in the United States of America

This portion of the story is dedicated to the children that make St. Patrick's Day the one day a year we can all be Irish.

CHAPTER ONE

CATCH ME IF YOU CAN

Racing quickly through the woods, Ethan followed only his instincts for where his next move should be.

Over the 10 months since his father had left on a mission to find the Mirror Men, Ethan had been working on his magical skills, and furthering his knowledge of his still very new, very exciting and sometimes dangerous vampyric gifts. He was beginning to understand the bond his kind had with nature and the connections needed to maintain survival of all species.

His mom had taught him to listen to the trees talk to one another, and feel the air warn him of potential danger or whisper of friends nearby. Even the river that ran behind his house carried visitors from far away, sharing their woes and triumphs with his backyard.

Listening was hard. He tried listening to the animals as they chattered, but he still couldn't quite care about hidden nuts and muddy hidey-holes. The crows complained the most, usually about how the humans were ruining everything. The squirrels constantly ranted and fussed with one other, just like Jeremy and Max did as brothers. He noted the similarity, and received an acorn to the head in response. Not so different from the schoolyard, he had laughed to himself.

He moved quickly from branch to branch, through the leaves, holding onto vines that entangled their way up the tree trunks. He was not going to get caught by his pursuers, not so close to home. The creatures had been chasing him for about a mile now. He was determined to either outsmart or outrun them and make it back to where Camille's father had set up a magical perimeter. Only then would he be safe and sound.

He saw it. The Whispering V, the prize was only 250 paces away; only 200 paces until he reached the boundary. Confidently, Ethan stopped on a tree limb and waited, smug in his accomplishment. Once he had contact with one of the pursuers, he took off in a race to the perimeter. Using his new-found skills, or maybe just adrenaline, he leaped around two trees, scrambled wildly across a broken, vine-covered branch and then... stopped dead in his tracks.

He was tangled in a spider web twenty feet from the ground and the creatures chasing him were nearly upon him. Carefully, he looked at the spider web. The Whispering V was only fifty paces away. If he could only get free, then in fifty paces he would have nothing to worry about. Ethan took a hard long gasp of air, preparing to tear away the sticky ropes. That's when he saw it... a spider, a really big spider. Strung up in her web, Ethan realized his life was about to end one way or another.

His pursuers paused just below him, relishing his defeat. They watched his futile struggle high above until suddenly their laughter broke the tension. The squirrels laughed in short staccato bursts, the sparrows tittered and flit about his head, the raccoons smirked and the deer snorted in true amusement. Even the trees rustled with mirth. Camille, Jeremy, Max, and Gretchen slipped from the shadows giggling and pointing.

"Why are you all laughing at me?" Ethan said quietly.

He knew that he had lost this challenge. In defeat, he was going to have to give all the animals treats. Worse, he would hear about his failure from his friends for some time to come.

"Help me down, please. Can't you see that this spider is going to feed me to her young?" Ethan's voice quivered in true fear.

"She is not going to hurt you; she is one-fifth your size. As a matter of fact, you could probably pick her up and move her off her web, then make your way down here yourself." Jeremy looked at Ethan curiously.

Camille and Gretchen giggled a little as they moved to climb up the tree.

"What's so funny?" Jeremy asked.

"You know what is funny, don't you Ethan?" Camille said, now only a few feet from him and the spider. Camille reached over and tapped Ethan on the shoulder.

"Caught you," she said.

Ethan still hadn't moved since he first saw the spider. It was like he was already cocooned in her web.

Out of nowhere, Max cried out, "Let Ethan down, he's good, let him down, let Ethan down now."

"It's alright Max, nothing bad is going to

happen to Ethan; we were just trying to teach him a lesson," Gretchen replied, breaking away the outer strands of webbing.

A young deer ambled closer to Max and rubbed up against him, while Jeremy grabbed his hand for reassurance.

"Thank you, Dawn, for helping us out here. I guess he has probably learned enough for this time." Camille reached over and Dawn the spider walked up her arm, over her shoulders and then back down her other arm to the tree beside them.

"It was my pleasure to assist you, my dear. He is a pretty good looking boy. I wouldn't mind having him tangled up in my web again," Dawn replied in a sultry, smooth voice as she ambled away.

The girls both giggled.

"You don't think I heard that, too? It is not funny and I am still stuck in this web up here," Ethan complained, knowing the more he moved the more tangled he would become.

"Come on Ethan," Jeremy yelled up at him.

"Come on down now Ethan. It is alright," Max echoed.

Looking at Camille, Ethan carefully freed one leg by pulling apart the web fiber. Making sure that he had enough web to hold onto, he kicked loose his other leg and swung over to a clear branch and then down. He stopped to regain his composure, and then shimmied his way down the trunk of the tree, muttering all the way.

Camille and Gretchen followed him with much less drama. Once on the ground, Ethan worked at taking the rest of the sticky, stringy web off of his clothes and out of his hair.

"What happened to you?" Jeremy asked as Max hugged Ethan tightly.

"Thanks Max," Ethan said as he rubbed Max's shoulder.

"I was almost there. I knew how far back you were and I knew the deer would have to maneuver around the trees and the squirrels would get distracted by the nuts that I planted in the tree limbs the other day. I thought I was home free," Ethan stated. "I didn't see any spider webs here before."

Both of the girls hadn't said a word. They waited to hear Ethan's version of the story.

"That spider was huge, it could have been a black widow or a red spotted widow or a tarantella!" Ethan declared, pretty sure of his words.

"That spider wasn't that big, and if it was

a poisonous spider than I am sure Camille would have stopped her from biting you." Jeremy looked at his friend in wonder.

"Oh come on, Ethan- tell Jeremy and Max the truth," Camille said.

"What is she talking about Ethan?" Jeremy asked.

"Alright, fine then I will tell you. I am scared of spiders. I don't care how big they are, how fuzzy they are, what color they are or if they are poisonous or not! They just weird me out, ok! My father always takes care of them and he tries to never kill them. He picks them up if they get in the house then places them outside. As far as I am concerned he could kill them and it wouldn't bother me!" Ethan replied, practically in one breath.

"How did a spider web get in your way, then? If you can't stand them I would think you would have thought that through too," Jeremy said to Ethan.

Ethan looked over at Camille and Gretchen, who were being far too quiet for such a great story.

"Alright I give!" Gretchen sighed, seeing his look. "I saw you get really weird about a spider at your house when my dad was here training you a few months ago. I thought it was pretty funny that a vampire kid would be scared of a little old harmless spider, so I told Camille."

Camille smiled at Ethan and looked at Jeremy, who was holding back from laughing out loud.

"But that doesn't explain how Dawn the spider was able to spin a web in the exact place that Ethan was going to cross today," Jeremy said, looking at Camille now, still holding back his laughter.

"That was all me," Camille stated proudly. "I had a vision last night of Ethan being chased, then stopping to kind of taunt his pursuers. I decided that was not really smart of him, so when we got here earlier I told Gretchen that I had a plan."

"So that is why you two ran out to the back earlier when we went inside." Ethan nodded, putting it all together now.

"I knew Dawn was a pretty feisty girl and that she would not be far off, you know keeping an eye on things and such. Gretchen and I went to look for the spot that I saw in my vision and then back-tracked a little. We showed Dawn the path that Ethan would probably take and well, the rest is history!" Camille replied with a smile.

No one said a word for a few minutes which could have been forever as far as Ethan was concerned. Finally Jeremy, not able to hold back any longer, started to laugh, then Camille and Gretchen followed suit. Only Max didn't laugh at Ethan.

Max said slowly, "That's not that funny Jeremy. You are scared of cockroaches."

"Hey! Why me? I didn't trap anyone," Jeremy protested, shaking his head at Ethan's snickering.

"You boys are so predictable, even when it comes to your moves. You are going to have to overcome your fear of spiders, Ethan. I am sure Dawn would love to help you with that!" Camille giggled and grabbed Gretchen's hand.

"Did you hear that?" Ethan interrupted.

"Hear what?" Jeremy replied.

Ethan smiled in relief; his mother had stepped out on the porch. Closing his eyes, he concentrated on the tiny vibrations of air. Using the gift of air talking, he moved the currents and directed them to ask her who was on the phone.

A moment passed and he felt the brush of her reply against his face. "You are getting the hang of this." The warmth of her smile tickled his nose.

Ethan appreciated the confidence in his mother's response. He had been working with Camille's father a lot on air talking, whisper speech or telepathy as this gift was called.

"You and your friends are going to have to come in from the woods to find out, and please turn the light out in the Whispering V before you do," she answered, returning to the house. She informed the caller that Ethan would be in shortly if they wanted to wait, and they did.

"It's my mom and she says that it is time for us to come in now. You guys can start on up, I have to turn the light off in the Whispering V first."

Three times in the past week Ethan had left the lights on in the Whispering V, and three times his mother had to go out and turn them off after Ethan had gone to bed. Ethan would not forget this time. His mother had told him last time that even if he was tired, he would have to go back into the woods if he forgot again.

Within minutes Ethan was in the house.

"STOP, right there Ethan and take off those dirty boots before walking in here!" his mother instructed him, standing with her arms folded firmly. "I have just cleaned this house for the fifth time this week and it is only Thursday."

"Alright, sorry. Don't you think that you are being a little obsessive about the cleaning, I mean... if it is only going to get dirty again in another day why not just wait till tomorrow?" Ethan suggested.

His mother just gave him that look as he leaned over to undo the laces and pulled off the boots with his toes. "If I had my own cell phone then I wouldn't have to come into the house and get it dirty at all," he thought out loud.

His mother just looked at him and thought, "Is this really the time for that discussion again?"

Hearing her thoughts loudly, he grumbled, "No, but..."

Dropping the boots outside the door onto the deck, his mother smiled at him as she held the phone with her hand cupped over it.

"Well, that was interesting," Jeremy said. "I'm glad my mother can't hear everything that I am thinking all the time!"

Jeremy's mother walked out the door before he finished his sentence.

"Oh really? So what is it that I didn't hear

you say, but you were thinking?" she asked, looking in Jeremy's direction.

"I will see you this weekend Helen," Senona continued. "Thanks for helping me with that new dress; it is gorgeous! Come on Jeremy, Max, Gretchen and Camille. It is getting late and you all have school tomorrow." She hugged Helen and stepped down the stairs towards the van.

"With this many kids to take home it is a good thing I didn't bring the broom," she joked while Helen shook her head.

Impatiently, Ethan looked at his mother. She still had the phone cupped in her hand.

"I hope that they are not paying for long distance," Ethan said as he reached for the phone.

"Remember I am your mother and not your personal assistant," she reminded him as she handed over the phone and walked away.

Ethan covered it with his hand and mouthed, "Mom, who is it?"

She turned. "Someone who must know your weaknesses. Now go inside and talk to them properly, so I can say good bye to Senona and the children."

Ethan walked back inside, waving goodbye to his friends as he did.

"Hello," Ethan said hesitantly. The voice on the other end of the line sounded like it was a million miles away.

"Hello Ethan. Patience is one of your biggest weaknesses and that will have to change."

Ethan seemed to stop breathing for a minute. "Dad... is it you really you?"

Ethan didn't know if he should start to dance or cry. His mother stopped him in mid-stride and told him he had to keep it down.

He hadn't spoken with his father on a phone since Yule, and that was cut short by a poor connection. He had communicated with him through a dream trance - another tool his mother had been teaching him - but it was still not the same.

"Yes, Ethan it is really me. Sorry about the bad connection again. I have difficulty finding land lines of any quality in this part of the world. Apparently, the technology goes into the mobile phones- which you have been trying to work out of your mother I hear."

Ethan was amazed that his father was on the phone with him after so long. He was more amazed that he could talk about anything other than the imprisonment of some of the others. False claims made by the government lead by the mirror men had led to the trials of many of their kind in recent months.

"Ethan are you still there, son?" his father asked, verifying their connection.

"Yes sir. I am here, it's just kind of weird to be really talking to you on the phone, even if the connection is not great," Ethan replied.

Ethan paused again, so his father continued to talk.

"So your mother has been keeping me up to date on most of the happenings around the house and school. Sounds like she is in a worried mood."

"You can tell that from talking with her?" Ethan asked.

Ethan's father laughed, creating a burst of static on the line. "No, son, I can tell that because she is cleaning every other day. I heard her tell you that while you were taking off your boots off. When you know someone really well you can tell their poker face. So, if she is cleaning as much as it sounds like she is than she is worried about something, or someone."

Ethan just listened, feeling the sound of his father's voice embrace him.

"Your mother told me that you were out in the woods working on your out-maneuvering skills. I would have thought that you knew those woods like the back of your hand by now," he teased gently, wanting his response.

"I do sir, but I was maneuvering through the woods twenty feet up in the trees, not touching the ground and at dusk!" Ethan told his father excitedly, proceeding to hit the highlights of the afternoon.

"Wow! That sounds like some intense training that Luis and your friends have been working on. I know your abilities and successes over the past year since you started to focus on training. I am confident you had no difficulties, son," his father acknowledged.

"Not really sir," Ethan confessed. "The woods are really wet and you can't really walk through them that well. It has rained a lot this past few months and it is so wet that some of the trees are worried that their roots are getting too weak. If the rain doesn't stop they may fall over or even get diseased. The creek has flowed over the dams for over twenty miles."

"Your mother told me about all the rain and that some rituals and other events have had to be held indoors. I did not realize that the heavy rain had started to uproot the trees in our woods, or that there was such a problem getting around in it! I am sorry to hear about that, Ethan. Please tell the trees that I am with them. They are strong and have seen this before," Ethan's father observed.

"I suppose this has given you a reason to work on developing some of your other new gifts and skills," he continued.

Ethan knew what his father was going to say next. "Yes sir, it has. I know you are going to say that everything happens for a reason."

His father's laughter echoed on the other end of the line as he replied, "Even though it has been almost a year since I have been face to face with you, we are still well-connected, son."

"Yes Dad, of course we are connected," Ethan agreed.

Ethan and his father had been in contact through visions while Ethan slept. It wasn't easy for Ethan to talk to him or really interact during this state, but he could feel his father's feelings and love for him. He knew that for the time being there was little chance that he was going to see him face to face. Not as long as he and the others were tracking the mirror men around the world.

"You said that there were not very many landline phones in the part of the world that you are in right now, Dad. Can you tell me where that is?" Ethan knew the answer but he also knew that his father was clever enough to give him a personal clue.

"You know that I can't tell you that son, to not endanger you and your mother. I sure do miss driving cars that can drift though," he told Ethan.

Ethan replied "Someday you will have to teach me some of those moves." He knew exactly where his father was and thought that was pretty cool, but a long way from home.

"I am going to have to go now; my friends here want to talk to their families too! Take care of your mother and keep up with your training, Ethan. Love you," his father said with the fatherly emotion in his voice that only Ethan would recognize.

"I love you too, Dad and don't worry about me. I am going to keep studying both in school and at home. I want to be just as strong, powerful and smart as you someday," Ethan asserted emphatically.

"Everyone here supports you and the

others in your pursuit," he continued, "and I know that you will find them and fixit - however you do that stuff!"

He realized that he wasn't sure exactly what his father and the others were going to do when they found the source of the mirror men, so he didn't really finish his entire thought.

"Give your mother a hug and kiss for me, please, and be good! Remember that this is not easy for her either, not having me around to share in the responsibilities. Also having the others around protecting the two of you leaves very little privacy. Work on the patience part of your training, too; it will serve you more than you will ever know."

"I will try, but it is hard you know," Ethan admitted as he hung up the phone.

CHAPTER TWO

WHAT A MORNING

Monday morning 5:45am. Ethan's alarm sounds over and over and over again. Ethan rolls over and hits the snooze button. 6:00 am the alarm sounds again. Ethan rolls over and hits it a second time. 6:15am Ethan rolls over to hit it again and the alarm clock is not there. He sits up thickly, disturbed and frustrated. Bleary, he looks around, then down on the floor beside his bed.

There, upside down with his one of his mother's cats lying on top of it was his poor alarm clock that had been taking a beating over the past half hour. He wasn't sure if he should laugh or be angry with Daisy. Then he saw Alix walk in the doorway.

"Oh, this is just great," Ethan thought to himself.

Daisy was known as the Queen by every

being in the house. Even Ethan's father referred to her as THE QUEEN. The name Daisy seemed strange for her, considering her attitude was not pretty or flowery. But apparently the only flowers that she wouldn't eat when she was younger were daisies, so hence the name.

She was old, so old that when someone asked, 'how old is the flame point cat', the response was always the same: 'quite old.' No one really ever remembered when she became the cat queen of the house. She paraded around the house like it was hers and hers alone, and everyone and everything else were barely tolerated guests.

She didn't allow anyone but Ethan's mother to touch her. Anyone who tried were surely going to have a few scratches, especially if she was sleeping. She would rather go and curl up under the covers in the guest room or sneak into Atticus' office and lay on his chair than to have to deal with silly people. On occasion she would allow visiting children to see her, amused by their efforts to sneak up and pet her soft reddish-orange and white fur. Prepared, she could turn quickly and draw just enough blood to remind them of their place. Other times she would allow the younger ones an occasional stroke, but repetition guaranteed that she would find a way to knock over a drink or steal snacks.

Ethan asked his dad once why he let her walk all over him and do mean things to their company.

He replied, "Son, there are just some things that are better left alone. As long as your mother is happy and Daisy is on our side, she can keep her throne."

His mom told him that the gods and goddesses trusted cats for their magical abilities, and suggested he do the same. Christian, a kid at school, said that his father told him that he couldn't ever have a cat because they weren't named in the bible. That meant they were evil, or something. His aunt once asked his mother to take Daisy on her personal yacht to help control rodents and pests. Like his mom would let Daisy go, even over one of their dead bodies.

Whatever the truth about cats and especially Daisy was, this morning it didn't matter. He had to hurry up or he would miss the school bus. Then someone would have to drive him to school, and his mother would not be happy.

Daisy didn't move a whisker as she

watched him, still upside-down on the alarm clock. Ethan sighed, seeing a black shadow slip through the door. Now he was going to have to deal with Alix. Over the years he had somehow become Daisy's warrior guard. Honestly everyone knew Daisy could handle things herself - especially Daisy. She enjoyed the intimidation factor of having a large, solid black stealth hunter by her side that would pounce the minute she let out a yowl.

Alix had shown up on their doorstep on Ethan's third birthday. Ethan liked him a lot so his mother had to invite the little black cat in. Since then, Alix had made an alliance with THE QUEEN and together they managed the household affairs.

Alix had moved in front of Ethan's dresser where he had his school clothes. Ethan did not want to start anything and jeopardize his dwindling chances of catching the school bus. He cautiously reached over Alix, grabbed the second drawer and opened it as quietly as he could. Daisy let out a low meow. Alix lifted and flicked his tail.

"Come on Alix, it's me Ethan, your favorite human/ vampire boy. Give me a break this morning. I have to hurry up and get ready for school," Ethan pleaded, knowing that he had only a slim chance of winning over Daisy. He wished that he had learned how to talk to animals like Camille and his mom. Then he could promise Alix that he would leave milk in his cereal bowl or something in exchange.

He slipped his shirt on gingerly, keeping one eye on Daisy and one on Alix, fearing that he may get a swat from one of them. So far so good, he thought to himself as he reached for his pants in the next drawer.

Again Daisy meowed, a little more insistently. This time Alix arched his back, staring at Ethan as he started to slip one leg into his pants. As he lifted his other leg, Alix jumped straight up, knocking Ethan off balance. He landed butt first on the floor. Not bothering to get up, Ethan pulled up the rest of his pant leg, giving Alix a look of disgust. Meanwhile, Daisy purred softly, like she had just won a beauty prize.

"Alright you three, enough joking around this morning." Ethan's mother stepped into the room to see Ethan lying on the floor, pants still undone. Daisy was still lying peacefully on the alarm clock, eyes half-closed while Alix groomed himself nonchalantly in front of Ethan.

"Thanks Mom, for rescuing me, I was just

trying to get ready for school when these two..."

Ethan was interrupted by his mother. "Enough with the talking Ethan, finish getting ready. Breakfast is on the table," his mother said, shaking her head at the three of them.

"Great, now she is mad at me and it was you two that started the whole thing. Thanks for nothing." Ethan walked to the bathroom and put on some deodorant of his father's that his mother had given him. He headed toward the kitchen, followed closely by Daisy and Alix.

"Yum, I smell great," Ethan said aloud. He did like the smell but he also was trying to make his mom smile like he promised his father.

"Since I was woken up twenty minutes early by someone's alarm, I figured I would make biscuits to go with your oatmeal for breakfast. Apparently someone didn't want get up this morning. Too big a weekend for you I suppose. Maybe we need to talk to Luis and Gregory about slowing down on your training while you are in school," his mother suggested, shaking her head.

"No Mom, I can do both. I have only dropped two percent in school you know; I am still on honor roll. I need to keep training to catch up to everyone else and be more prepared to protect you while Dad's away. Please, Mom," Ethan begged.

"I have to be better prepared for my share of the responsibilities around here and in the community with the others."

She looked at him long and hard as she sipped slowly on her coffee, watching as Ethan devoured his breakfast. She knew that he was trying to read her thoughts, but she shielded from him very well. She sat her coffee down and tucked her robe more tightly around her. She reached down and picked up Daisy who had made her way into the kitchen and was now rubbing on her leg.

"I will have to think about the training. If your school grades drop any more or if you continue to have problems getting out of bed in the mornings then I am going to suspend your training. After all, you are only 10 years old and you will have plenty of time to train later," she told him as she stroked Daisy's fur.

Daisy looked at him, blinking her eyes in emphasis. Ethan looked back at her with a menacing grin that didn't even make her flinch.

"Alright you two, enough with your little

games," Ethan mother scolded as she reached for her coffee cup.

"But Mom, Daisy and Alix were the ones that slowed me down this morning and made me miss the bus." Ethan tried to look as innocent as possible.

"The way I see it Ethan, if it weren't for Daisy coming into your room and knocking the alarm off the table in the first place you still wouldn't be out of bed. Then you would be late for school and not just missing the bus. As a matter of fact, you know how Daisy hates getting up before you leave for school in the morning. You are lucky that is all that she did. She could have climbed into your bed and woken you up herself." Ethan knew his mom had a point, so he smiled in defeat and turned his head toward his book bag as if he was ready to leave.

"You will have to wait for me to get one of Luis' men to drive you to school my dear. I hope that this is a lesson for you." She paused, waiting for a response from Ethan. Ethan looked in her direction and reluctantly nodded.

"Yes, Mom, you are right. I should have got up after the first snooze alarm. Please don't stop or slow down my training, though.

I beg you, PLEASE give me another chance, PLEASE!"

She knew that begging meant he was truly paying attention. A rap on the front door startled them both and they jumped hastily out of their chairs. So busy were they discussing training that they had not realized someone had approached the house.

"Did you call someone to pick me up, already?" Ethan asked as he walked towards the door.

"No, but I don't feel any danger at the door", his mother replied cautiously, scanning the energy surrounding the house.

A large man stood on the porch just outside the door. He appeared to Ethan to be 7 feet tall with shoulders 4 feet wide. He didn't say a word as he stood there and motioned for Ethan to follow him. Neither Ethan nor his mother moved a muscle. They were not familiar with the man, even though he didn't appear to pose any threat to them.

The phone rang. Ethan turned to his mother for approval to go back to the kitchen to get the phone; she smiled and nodded, still holding the door.

"Good morning, Ethan." The voice on other end of the phone was Jeremy's dad.

"Hi sir, uh, we have a situation here at the house right now," Ethan replied.

"Oh, I am sorry. He must be there already. I was having a hard time getting a signal for this new mobile phone. The man at your door is one of my very good friends from the old country. He doesn't speak at all. Would you put your mother on the phone, please?"

"Yes sir," Ethan replied, reassured. He was already walking in her direction, and handed the phone over to his mother.

"It is Jeremy's dad, he knows this man," Ethan told his mother.

"Good Morning Luis. This has been an interesting beginning to the day," she said.

"I do apologize for this situation, Helen. I tried to call, but this new phone service is on again, off again," Luis explained. "Madera is a very good friend and very loyal to our kind. I invited him from the old country to assist with security. He has been watching you and Ethan for a few weeks and noticed that Ethan did not get on the bus this morning. Is there a problem?"

"The problem is that Ethan didn't want to get up this morning, Alix and Daisy took matters into their own hands, I got up too early and there is a 7 foot giant at my front door that won't talk to me," Helen replied, irritated.

"I hear you Helen, sounds like a full day before 7:30am. My friend Madera cannot speak. He will make sure that Ethan gets to school safely; his car is down the road." Louis replied.

"Alright Luis, but it would have been nice if I knew who you have watching over us!"

"It is for your own safety that we try to keep them in the shadows as much as possible," he reminded her. "I will have to have a talk with Ethan for messing up the schedule and causing additional issues," Luis added.

"Oh, I have already informed him that this cannot become a regular occurrence or his training will be suspended," she informed Luis.

"I am sorry if Madera shocked you in any way, my lady," Luis replied. "Ethan had best hurry if he is not to be late for school today."

"Yes I suppose he will be late if he doesn't leave now. Oh, another thing - would you have Senora give me a call after I have my coffee this morning? I need her help with something," Helen added.

"Certainly Helen, enjoy your coffee," Luis agreed.

Helen returned to the front foyer of the house to remind Ethan it was time to go. When she got there, she saw Madera lifting Ethan up and down with only one hand, like he was curling a barbell.

"Check this out Mom! No one is going to mess with us if we have Mr. Madera here. He is super strong." Ethan shouted breathlessly.

She shook her head and rolled her eyes.

"Yes, he does seem quite strong. However I think Mr. Madera would agree that strength of the body is one thing, but the strength of the trilogy, Mind, Body and Soul is much stronger over all," Ethan's mother observed.

With that, Madera deposited Ethan on his feet and lowered his head a few degrees, not completely understanding what she had just said but recognizing that it was not his place to argue or agree.

"You're right Mom, I know, it is just that he is so big and well..." Ethan was stopped mid-sentence by his mother.

"School! It is time for you to go to school now or you will be late." His mother reminded him firmly.

Ethan started to walk out the door, following about 40 feet behind the large structure of Madera.

"Ethan!" His mother yelled out to him. Are you forgetting something?"

Ethan thought for a moment, then heard it in his mother whisper, "Your school bag, lunch and project are still on the table." She had been shaking her head a lot this morning already and it was only an hour into the day.

He sighed and ran back to the house, slipping by his mother in the doorway and grabbing his bag off the table. On the way back out he stopped, looked at his mother with an impish smile, gave her a little kiss, and told her he would brush them as soon as he got home.

She sighed and laughed, shaking her head as she walked back into the house to have that coffee she needed so badly.

CHAPTER THREE

ONE OF THOSE DAYS

Later that morning, Helen received a call at work from Gregory, Camille's father. He did not sound like himself, so Helen asked him to wait a minute while she closed her lab door. Gregory was a very wise and knowledgeable man, who rarely spoke on any topic that he did not know well or that he did not study before discussing. These reasons alone would explain why he was such a strong seer and had such firm knowledge of the mystic world. There were only a few topics that he did find difficult and one of them was Camille.

"I am here," Helen informed Gregory as she raised the phone from the desk to her ear.

"I do hate to trouble you at work Helen. However I have a few concerns with Camille. I am not sure how to deal with this situation or even if I need to at this time. I was going to wait until later but I don't want to miss my opportunity to work with my daughter first," Gregory said with such concern that Helen felt his worry draping him like a shroud.

"We are family Gregory. You have given so much of your time and energy in training Ethan. I will do whatever I can to help you with Camille," Helen assured him. She knew that Gregory was in need of someone to listen as he worked through his thoughts. "I know that you are trying so hard to raise her on your own since the incident. I am sure that can be very trying at times." She stopped talking and listened to his breathing, picking up only on the peace that he was trying to maintain.

"I suppose that I have been in need of additional assistance with the care of Camille. I believe that she is not yet ready to move past the issues that we have had with her mother and sister. I am pleased that her gifts are developing but I am also afraid. I am afraid that as she grows stronger she will realize more of the truths and secrets that we have been able to protect our children from over the years. I knew that these days would come, but I just thought that I would be better prepared for them. She could have been more distracted with boys or fashion," he lamented, followed with a little chuckle.

"I know there is something else bothering you," Helen observed, waiting to hear the real reason for his call.

Silence rested on the phone line as Gregory collected his thoughts. He was momentarily unsure if he should burden Helen with his personal concerns.

He cleared his throat and continued, "The last few times that we have sat together to discuss school and other activities she has been blocking me out of her head and her thoughts. It is not like Camille, to not tell me things. We have always been very open with each other and shared both the good and the bad with each other, in that father-daughter kind of way.

"When she was at your place this weekend did you pick up on anything out of the ordinary?"

Helen thought carefully about everything that he had just told her. She honestly could not think of anything that was out of the ordinary.

"I am sorry Gregory, but I didn't feel that Camille was in any way acting different with me, Senona or any of the other children. As a matter of fact, she and Gretchen were acting quite giddy - pulling practical jokes on the boys," Helen replied, laughing a bit thinking of how they got Ethan at his own game.

"I may just be over-reacting. I sense that something is going on with her, but I cannot figure it out." Gregory sighed.

Helen once again cracked a hint of a smile as she replied.

"Gregory, I am sure that I don't need to remind you that she is still a girl hitting her pre-teen years. I don't have a daughter but I do know that young women these days do have a little bit more drama in their lives than when you or I were younger. Between the semi-reality T.V. shows they watch, the moody love stories they read, and the multimedia devices they have attached to their finger tips, it is amazing any of them ever survive this age. " Helen stopped for a second to make sure that Gregory was still listening.

"I am still here," Gregory replied. "I suppose I never really looked at it that way. I am not as familiar with all the new T.V. shows, books and games out there unless they affect our community; there are plenty that do." He paused for a moment and an eerie silence crept over the phone line. Helen knew what he was thinking, but he wouldn't talk about it.

"I know Gregory," she replied into the deep silence. "It has to be hard for you to have to take care of issues in the community, take care of your business and have to deal with a pre-teen girl - all on your own. You know that if Sofia were able to come back and help that she would have all this under control with you. We all miss her, but you know it has to be this way." Helen stopped herself. She knew that if she kept on that subject with him then it would only make him feel worse.

"So you feel that she may just be a little consumed by the mainstream media, technology, pop music and boys? It is not anything too serious then," he mused.

"More than likely she is just growing up and trying to fit into both worlds, since neither one is really ready to accept the other one yet. It is a lot easier to follow their rules than it is to follow ours! I will try to tap into her the next time I see or talk with her; I believe she will be attending Max's birthday party at Senona and Luis' in a few weeks. I will also ask Ethan carefully how Camille and the others are doing with their studies," she offered.

Before Gregory could respond, Helen added, "I don't think boys are an issue yet, though. Camille seems way too interested in world events to have to deal with a personal relationship with anyone except you or Lilith. Does that sound familiar?" Helen asked.

Gregory laughed. "Thank you, Helen, for being there for Camille. I thought I should tell you that Ethan is doing quite well with his training and will do better once he can stay focused a little more. I realize that he is still a little younger than the others, but he has amazing gifts. I know what the prophets have said and I am very encouraged."

"With Atticus tracking these Mirror Men and only making it home for a week here and there, I have been worried. Ethan could want to learn too much on his own or maybe even reject his gifts and well..."

Gregory stopped her, saying that there was no chance with his genes that he would ever reject anything but pea soup.

"Thank you Gregory, and we will talk more later about the children," Helen replied, saying goodbye with a smile.

Shortly after getting off the phone with Gregory, the phone rang again.

"Hello, Senona," Helen answered.

"Oh, did I catch you at a bad time?" Sonora replied.

"No, I had the phone right beside me and everyone has left for lunch, so this is as good a time as any," Helen replied with some hesitation in her voice, wondering at how long this day was becoming.

CHAPTER FOUR

THE DRAGON

Halfway through the day, the school bell signaled lunch time for Ethan and the other students. Ethan couldn't have been happier. He had been sitting in language arts class for the last three hours. He had to listen to other students read the stories that they had written about their favorite animals. That was the topic of this week's assignment, to develop a story and characters about your favorite animal.

Ethan was not really excited about this topic, and he had to present his story to the class right after lunch. He found a seat in the cafeteria to eat his lunch that included a tuna sandwich with a little mustard, blueberry muffin, half an apple and a drink bottle with rasp-cranberry punch his mom had told him he had to start drinking.

He couldn't help but think that he would have rather presented his story last week about the super volcano that erupted after a gas line pipe exploded. Now *that* was a great story. As he ate, he talked with his friends and listened to others at the table discuss their cats, dogs, fish, birds and even snakes. All he could think about was how bored he was already, listening to the other students read aloud their spoiled pet stories. They would dress them up, paint their nails, let them finish the table scraps, let them take baths with them and sleep with them. He hadn't heard about any of the animals going to the pet doctor, going running with them, or protecting them from intruders like his pets did.

He snickered to himself, imagining telling them how his day had started with Daisy and Alix. The only story that was of any interest to Ethan at all was by one of the girls who wrote about how her cat was a predator. She told them how her cat would prowl along the walls sensing some danger in or behind them. When the timing was just right, the cat would pounce on a mouse or bug that had taken a chance and challenged the cat for some table scraps left over on a plate or cat food hidden behind a door. Ethan thought that she, at least, had a pretty useful animal story. Still, he thought the whole assignment was to write about your favorite animal, not your favorite pet stories.

When lunch was just about over one of the kids punched Ethan in the shoulder and said, "Hey dude try to keep your story short. I don't want to fall asleep again and get in trouble for snoring."

Some of the kids at the table laughed, but Ethan bit his tongue and smiled as he picked up his things, packed them back into his lunch bag and got up from the table. He didn't really like the kid all that much and didn't want to do or say anything that he would have to explain later.

A girl came up behind him and told him that she enjoyed listening to his stories even if they seemed a little odd. He sort of thanked her by nodding his head and flicking his hair back. Before he could say a word she darted into the girl's bathroom as they passed it.

Ethan was always a bit of a storyteller, even before he found out about his part in the magical world. He had enjoyed writing and telling fantasy stories about wizards, dragons, vampires, sharks, natural disasters and environmental hazards. He even wrote a few songs that he would sing loudly while improvising with his guitar.

Like his father, he was known to elaborate a little more than he probably needed to, just to finish his idea. Keeping a journal had helped him organize his thoughts and even his spelling was improving.

Back in class, after another student told his story about his favorite animal, (which happened to be his hamster), it was Ethan's turn to share his assignment. He gathered his papers and approached the front of the class; he placed one copy on the teacher's desk so she could make corrections as she followed along. Ethan cleared his throat, took a deep breath and started his introduction.

"My favorite animal is the dragon, and my story is called, 'What really happened to the Dragon'."

One of the kids interrupted, "There is no such thing as dragons, so how can you write about a dragon?"

The teacher quieted the class. Ethan asked him how he knew there were no such things as dragons. The boy replied that his father had told him that they were just myths to scare people.

Ethan retorted, "Well, there were and probably still are dragons, just like there are giant squids, stink bugs and two-headed snakes. Someday, like a thousand years from now, people will say there was no such thing as elephants, white tigers or whales if we keep killing them."

"Ok Ethan," the teacher stated, "I think you have made a valid argument. I never said that it had to be a domestic animal. So let's continue, please."

When Ethan finished his story, which took 30 minutes to tell, most of the kids were staring at him. Actually, once he was in the second paragraph everyone was listening so intently that a pin drop could have been heard in the classroom. The teacher moved her chair out from behind her desk and stood up.

"Class, that is what I would like all your stories to sound like. The characters were well-developed, and the beginning and end flowed together seamlessly. Thank you, Ethan, for that incredible story about the prince and the dragon. If I didn't know better, I would have thought you knew him personally," she added, as the class applauded.

The same boy laughed loudly and said, "It may have sounded good, but it is still stupid.

Only a 4-year-old would read a book about dragons."

"Well, I must be 4 years old, then," a voice said from behind him. "I just finished the first of three books about a dragon and I am excited to start the next one."

A slight, dark-haired boy slouched in his seat at the back of the room. Gabriel was a new friend of Ethan's that Gretchen had introduced to him at the Black Eyed Peas concert. The argumentative boy turned around in his seat to face this new challenger, when suddenly he screamed in pain and launched himself out of his chair. He was hopping around, patting his pants that appeared to be smoking.

"My butt is on fire, my butt is on fire!" he screamed.

Irritated, the teacher walked briskly to where he was jumping around. Grabbing his arm, she said, "I have had enough of your games today. Playing with a lighter in class has earned you a visit to the office."

Stunned to silence, the rest of the class sat remarkably still as she ushered the disruptor out of the classroom.

A small grin played on Ethan's lips as he took his seat. He glanced at Gabriel a little uncertainly. Gabriel returned the look with a slight raise of his left eyebrow.

"Alright class, that was enough excitement for today," the teacher announced briskly upon returning. "The next student to disrupt my class will go directly to ISS. Now, we have one story left before the end of the day, so let's move along."

After class, Ethan caught up with Gabriel in the hall as they made their way to their designated bus areas.

"Hey Gabriel, thanks for bringing up the dragon book series that you are reading. Not too many kids read as much as you, so that was really great!" Ethan said, nodding his head.

"Yeah no problem Ethan," Gabriel replied. "I kind of liked your story and I don't like that kid. It was a little lame on the violence and destruction part, though. More of that would have made it really cool. You know, dragons are a little more dangerous than you made them out to be, right?"

Gabriel smiled and added, "I really liked the fact that the dragon started a fire under his butt. That's the way to put him in the hot seat!"

Ethan thought for a moment, trying to

remember what Gretchen had said about Gabriel. Or maybe she just said that she wanted to tell him something, but never got around to it.

"Yeah that was pretty funny!" Ethan agreed. Could Gabriel have done that, or was it just a coincidence that he was playing with a lighter?

Ethan thought for a moment, choosing his words carefully. "Well, it wasn't really about killing and all that stuff. I guess if it were I would have to add a girl needing help as well."

They both laughed as they continued down the hall, practically dragging their book bags.

"I got to go; this is my bus. Maybe we can hang out sometime and do something?" Ethan suggested, waiting a minute for Gabriel to answer him.

Then he heard his thoughts '...I wonder if Gretchen would be there too? Then I would really want to hang out with him...'

Quickly, Ethan added, "I mean only if you don't mind if Gretchen, Camille and Jeremy hang out with us too. I know some parents don't like if there are girls and boys together outside of school."

Gabriel replied "Sounds great; of course I will have to ask my parents, but yeah, I think that would be cool!" Gabriel and Ethan bumped fists and he turned towards his bus staging area as Ethan walked away.

On the way home on the bus, Ethan thought about the other kids' stories. If they only knew what he knew about all the other things in the world that really existed. Ethan had never seen a real dragon himself, but his father and other elders talked about them often. After all, if vampires, witches, fairies, ghosts, gargoyles and mirror men were real, then dragons had to be real, too.

CHAPTER FIVE

QUESTIONS, QUESTIONS

L ater that evening, after Ethan had returned home from his guitar lesson, his mother asked him how his day went. She knew that something was troubling him. Normally she would be able to sense his thoughts and help him out, but between her nerves and his emotions she was not able to piece it together.

"Fine, I guess," Ethan replied, which didn't mean much coming from a 10-year-old, of course. Ethan moped his way into the kitchen for a snack and drink before he sat down to his homework. He was not even going to argue about doing it, considering the way the day started.

"Did the teacher enjoy your story about dragons? I am sure the kids really liked it," she tried, hoping to get him to open up about what was going on in his head.

"Yeah, I guess the teacher liked it. She told everyone that was how she wanted all their stories written, so I guess that was good and bad." Ethan wasn't sure if having his writing singled out was good for his friendships or not.

"Of course that is good, Ethan. I am so proud of you, and Senona read it and enjoyed it, too. I always felt that you had some of the bard in you like your father." She smiled encouragingly.

"What is a bard, Mom?" Ethan asked.

She knew that if she used a word that he wasn't familiar with but was interested in, he would continue the conversation.

"Well, it is an older word for a person that is a writer and poet. You know how your father tells his stories around the fire or at the table? That is what a bard used to do in the old days. You have to remember, Ethan, not long ago very few people could read or write. A few people in town would tell stories of the past and recount the news of the day. If memory serves me well, I believe the tradition originated in Ireland and Scotland. I think that is what your father told me; of course I am not as old as he is so I don't remember them myself," she said, laughing.

"It must have been pretty cool to be able to read and write anything that you wanted to and not have kids questioning everything or laughing at you," Ethan commented.

"You would have enjoyed it very much, Ethan. I remember a few years ago the story that your father told you about how mosquitoes came to be. You retold that story a hundred times to anyone that would listen. So, were some of the kids in your class critical of your story today?"

"Most of the kids did their assignments on dogs and cats, which I thought was very boring. I could have done mine on dogs and cats, but the teacher *said* our favorite animal, not our pet, so I chose the dragon. First, they told me not to talk too long, and then they said that dragons don't exist. But I read my story and everyone listened and didn't even move.

"Then this kid yelled out 'only babies read dragon stories.' It made me mad because they are real and they are probably still around. I saw a dragon in one of my dreams and it was definitely not pretend." Ethan took a sip of his drink and a handful of dry cereal before he continued.

"A boy in my class named Gabriel stood up and said he must be a baby because he was reading a book series about dragons. Everyone laughed and the teacher told them to stop so she could continue. Oh yeah, and a fire started under that kid's butt, the one who was making fun of my story. I know I didn't do it - not to say I wouldn't have if I could, but I didn't."

Stopping again to take a sip of his drink he smiled at his mom.

"Do you think dragons are real, Mom?" Ethan asked.

"I know they are real Ethan; there are all kinds of dragons around the world. I have heard your father discuss dragons with zoologists, dragonologists and skeptics alike. His argument is simple. Before the internet, before ships crossed the sea, before automobiles, trains and airplanes, images of dragons were found in every culture on every continent. People who never met, or even knew of the existence of each other, described similar creatures with only minor differences. They even shared similar myths, which can only mean dragons are real. Where they are now is another story. I am sure your father will share that with you someday," she concluded, as Ethan considered her logic intently.

"Thanks, Mom. That makes me feel better. It's just hard sometimes to understand what is real, when so many people don't seem to know the difference. Like the other day, some boys were arguing about the best WWE wrestlers. The girls are always talking about Hanna Montana, and how she shouldn't be so mean to her friend. Like that is real!

"I was wondering if I could invite Gabriel over to the house sometime. There is something about him I like. I think we could be pretty good friends someday."

"I don't see why not," his mom agreed. "If you get his phone number, I will talk to his parents. These next few months are going to be very busy, so we'll have to squeeze it in. Max's birthday is next week, and St. Patrick's Day lands on a Friday this year, so that will be a big weekend. I know you are ready for a few busy months, if you can get out of bed," she teased, "but how are Jeremy, Gretchen and Camille? Are they excited?" she probed.

"They are all looking forward to everything. Jeremy is excited because everyone is coming to his house for Max's birthday and St. Patrick's Day. Gretchen is happy because she is off grounding, finally. This year, I will understand everything better and get to play some of the games you wouldn't let me play last year," Ethan explained.

"I am glad you are all excited; you should be," his mother replied.

Ethan stood and gave her a hug, sensing something still on her mind. "I better get this homework done so I have time to meet up with the others in the Serenity Channel," Ethan said, sitting back down at the table.

"Good idea," she agreed, ruffling his hair like his father would. She turned and began preparations for dinner, wondering why Ethan hadn't mentioned Camille.

CHAPTER SIX

PART 1

PRE-BIRTHDAY FUN

Birthdays are a big deal to all children; however, for the children of the others they were an even bigger event. Not because the gifts were more exciting, or that they could get away with just about anything, but because only so many years were allotted to learn and grow before being handed the responsibility for many of the traditions and family secrets. Fortunately for some of the younger children, the Elders had raised the age for maturity, which granted a few more years of freedom before they, too, accepted the duty of their destiny.

Ethan's father Atticus, although one of the old world vampires, had married and created a blood line with Helen, a new world vampire. She had helped to enlighten him on the changes in the world and see where the old ways were falling short of their ideals for the younger generation.

Atticus petitioned the other Elders of the councils to drop some traditions and modernize others, including when children came of age. He argued that the youth of today were working less on farms, merchant trading, shipping, carnivals, and as travelling musicians. This meant that they were staying home longer and developing socially and physically more slowly. Not that their growth wasn't encouraged, but this new world didn't need them to develop as quickly.

Helen had explained this to Atticus over and over when he wondered why it took so long for the children to understand his train of thought. The rapid advances in technology and the changes in social behavior, starting with the telegraph machine, then the telephone and now mobile communication and computers brought everything to their finger tips. They didn't have to travel to see the world, go to the theatre to listen to music, or attend social gatherings to converse with their peers. Farming with machines rather than mules eliminated the dependence on children for labor. After more than two decades, changes were adopted, including the timing of Atticus' own talk with Ethan.

Birthdays were one of changes that all the children were very happy about. Coming of age was once the 12th year of life. At that time, work and starting a family was expected. Atticus had suggested that the coming of age be changed to the 18th year of birth, to reflect the norms of modern life. However, the council of elders finally agreed on the 16th year. That point marked the near-ideal development of the body, when some children would start slowing down in the aging process, while still others would evolve more rapidly. Still, even four more years of birthdays seemed a good thing to any kid.

"Jeremy, have you cleaned your room and taken the trash out? And are the pets fed and...," his mom yelled from the second floor of the house.

"Yes, it's all done and I put the Piñata stick away too!" he yelled back. Two years ago he had left the Piñata stick out and Max had smashed it open before the party had even started.

"You're a big help Jeremy and a great big

brother," she said as she came floating down the stairs.

"Mom, you may want to watch the hovering thing: you know that not everyone here is witch friendly," Jeremy cautioned, smiling at Max who had just grabbed his hand.

"Oh, Jeremy you're right. I just got a little behind with the rewrite that had to be finished this morning and I thought a little magic wouldn't hurt," she replied, sounding like a contrite 10 year old.

She gave Max and Jeremy a group hug, then whizzed by them towards the kitchen to check the food in the oven. She then darted into the pantry to make sure the cake was still intact, and seeing that it was, she let out a giggle. Everyone, including the animals, knew to stay out of her way when she was whizzing around on a mission, to avoid being knocked over.

"Oh my baby Max is turning 8 years of age today," she chanted out loud as she exited the pantry. "I get so excited over birthdays; I just can't help myself from being happy!"

Jeremy looked down at Max, shook his head and then rolled his eyes, as if to say, REALLY WE COULDN'T TELL.

To top things off, she walked back through

the sitting room where Jeremy and Max were still standing and gave them both big kisses.

"Ah Mom, did you have to? You have lipstick all over us now, and worse, it tastes and smells like strawberries," Jeremy grunted.

Senona just smiled and scurried off, humming some Spanish lullaby that she sang to them when they were babies. It was still hard for Jeremy to get mad at her when she started to sing in Spanish. He was convinced that she put some Spanish lullaby spell on them when they were little.

"Dad, are we glad you are home early. Mom is going all birthday weird on us," Jeremy complained as his dad came in the door. Luis took off his boots and jacket and placed them in the closet.

"You boys are looking great, all cleaned up and ready for the party. Oh, I can see your Mother has been sharing some love with you." He placed his huge hands on their faces and rubbed the lipstick smears off the side of their mouths. "I knew that your Mom would be in her sweet, love mood today, but it looks and sounds like she is overdosing on it," he observed quietly, so only the boys could hear. The lullaby echoed through the house liltingly, creating a surreal sense of peace.

Luis continued in an exaggerated Latin accent, "Don't you boys worry, I am home for the rest of the day and I will keep your mom occupied so you won't have to worry about strawberry lipstick until bedtime. I will have her place all her kisses on me, her Latin lover."

Both the boys shook their heads and stared at their father in dismay as he worked his charm.

"Now you boys run off and play until our guests arrive. Go... have fun, but don't touch the cake or Piñata! I shall have your mother surrender herself to me, her Latin gargoyle lover!"

"Really, did you have to go there with the whole lover thing? It's just TMI, Dad," Jeremy groaned as Luis hoisted Max up with one hand and Jeremy with the other to hug them into his chest. Jeremy always liked when his father gave him beargoyle hugs, as they called them. He could smell a hint of sweat under the scent of fresh cut lumber.

Even though his father now owned his own construction company, he still liked to get out and get dirty. While many home builders were going bankrupt, Luis' company was still going strong. A few years ago Gregory had foreseen a downturn in the housing industry. Luis had just bought out his boss five years earlier and couldn't afford to lose any business. Atticus recommended that Luis change with the times and go green from the ground up. He started making changes to his designs, going to eco-friendly seminars, reeducating his clientele and working to LEED standards.

Even with the higher upfront costs, Luis had more clients wanting his business and just as many subcontractors wanting to work for him. Within just two years, the changes he made, such as spray foam insulation, geothermal heating and cooling, solar shingles and recycled materials had situated his company as a leader in providing quality and durability. He now ran four crews in a 100 mile radius, with a two year backlog in business.

Saturdays he would do trim carpentry, a little flooring or even some framing. On occasion, Jeremy would go out with him. He would clean up a jobsite or do a little painting and even pull some wires for a subcontractor if someone didn't show up. His payment was a 12" sub sandwich, a few bad jokes from the contractors and $20.00 at 2 pm.

Truth was that Jeremy liked going out

and watching his dad work. He could feel the respect his people had for him and he for them. He enjoyed listening to his dad's Spanish charm with the lady home owners and seeing his strength as he carried loads of wood and panels up the ladders to the roof.

"Way too much romance for me," Jeremy said after his dad put them down and followed his mom upstairs. He looked at Max and shook his head again.

"I like it Jeremy," Max replied. "Mommy and Daddy love each other and you and me!"

"Duh, I know they do. But do they have to do all that mushy stuff in front of us?" Jeremy grumbled as he went into the pantry to check out Max's cake.

"Nice cake," he said to Max as he pretended to put a finger in it.

Max knew that he wouldn't really put his finger in it so he just ignored him, but he did still keep an eye on him. He might be getting the pre-teen disease that he heard his Mom and Dad talking about. Other kids had gotten it as they got closer to being teenagers.

Max followed Jeremy into the family room where they had their Playstation game system. Jeremy plopped down on the oversized couch and Max followed suit. Jeremy picked up one of the controllers and Max picked up the other. Jeremy already had one of the Star Wars games in the system from earlier that morning.

"You can't play this game, little brother. There is too much information for you to keep up with," Jeremy informed Max.

Truth was that Max was better at the game than Jeremy because he didn't lose focus as easily. Jeremy always tried to psyche out Max so that he would get further ahead in the beginning, and when Max did get his head in the game Jeremy would still stand a chance. Usually, Max kicked his butt before they had to stop playing.

They played the game and horsed around, waiting to hear the doorbell ring or Spartan bark, whichever came first. Finally, the doorbell chimed and Spartan barked furiously. Not that Spartan was going to do much if someone did open the door, but it sounded threatening enough.

Jeremy jumped up and ran to the front door, yelling, "I got it, Mom, don't worry," as Max followed steps behind. Jeremy flung open the door to see Camille and Gretchen.

"Hey baby, you are such a good boy. Protecting us from big, bad, terrible monsters," they cooed as they stepped in and started to play with Spartan.

"Hey what about us, we were here, too. You could have been Mirror Men or something strange," Jeremy said, looking down at the girls now on the floor playing with Spartan. Max was not interested in presumptive bad guys, so he was on the floor with Spartan and the girls.

"I am sure you would have conjured some kind of troubling spell to scare them away," Camille replied soothingly, looking up at Jeremy with an impish smile on her face.

"Oh yeah, well how..ah.. do we know that you two aren't Mirror Men in disguise or evil zombies, hmm?" Jeremy was a little frustrated, although he suspected that they were messing with him the way girls will with boys.

"Really, Jeremy," Gretchen said, shaking her head at him. "Do you think that Spartan would be rolling around on his back on the floor and letting us rub his belly if we were some evil bad guys? Don't you think Max would know if we were disguised Mirror Men? Anyway, no bad guys could ever be as good at messing with your head as we are," Gretchen concluded smugly.

"Happy Birthday, Max," Camille said, giving him a hug. Max smiled at Jeremy as he looked out from under Camille's arm.

"Hey, Jeremy," a voice said from behind him. It was Ethan and he was carrying a Tupperware container full of some kind of food. He was followed by Helen, who also had her arms full of stuff, including what looked like some presents. Then behind her was another person that had to duck to get through the doorway.

"Have you guys met Madera before?" Ethan asked Jeremy and Max. Before Jeremy could even answer, Ethan continued. "He is one of your people - well sort-of people, I guess. Your dad has him watching over us for a while. I guess he thinks that we are not yet ready to take on the Mirror Men by ourselves."

He lowered his voice to a confidential whisper. "He told me was tortured and got his tongue cut out a long time ago, which is why he can't talk."

Impressed, Jeremy looked up, way up, at Madera as he made his way through the doorway. He seemed somewhat familiar to Jeremy, but he wasn't sure. He waited for the hulking man to place the bags down that

Helen had him carrying, then introduced himself.

"I am Jeremy, son of Luis Valentia. It is a pleasure to meet you sir," Jeremy said as he lowered his head, then raised his hands to Madera's.

"He says that he last saw you when you were only a few weeks old. You were a good looking baby and now you are a good looking young man." Ethan had worked out a system of relaying messages from Madera since he could read some of his thoughts.

The girls laughed at the idea of Jeremy being a good-looking anything. "Is he sure that Jeremy is the same boy as the baby he knew 11 years ago?" Camille asked.

Madera leaned into Jeremy and took a deep breath.

"You don't really have to check, sir," Ethan said looking up at Madera and frowning at Camille. "Girls like to make JOKES about us boys. They know that you wouldn't make such a mistake."

"With all due respect sir, I am sorry. It is just too easy for us to pick on Jeremy and Ethan." Camille apologized to Madera as Helen walked back into the foyer looking for Ethan and Madera, who still had the bags and

Tupperware that had to go into the dining room.

"Alright, that will be enough for now. We still have a birthday party here today for a very special birthday boy," Helen said as she reached down gave Max a hug and kiss. "At this age Madera, the girls are a little smarter than the boys so they find it easy to aggravate them."

"Is that you Helen?" Senona yelled as she once again glided down the staircase. "Oh I am so happy you all are here."

"I can see that you are in your happy mood. You may want to be careful with using your magic there, my dear," Helen chided gently as Senona floated towards her to kiss her on the cheek.

"I already told her that," Jeremy interrupted, "but she and Dad are well, you know, in that Latin lover happy place. That means all bets are off as to whether or not she will use it in front of the ungifted guests."

"Thank you, Jeremy. Now you can leave that up to us and you guys can go do your thing while we talk and keep an eye on this love bird," Helen replied.

Senona whipped through the kitchen and pantry, confirming that everything was in its place. She then greeted Madera with a big hug. He hesitated a little, and stood awkwardly in her embrace. Too busy to notice, she grabbed Helen's hand to drag her up the stairs to help her finish getting dressed. Madera left the room, knowing that his responsibility was to keep watch from the shadows. Soon the house would be full of guests and his duties would begin.

The children ran off to the other room. They reminded Max of some of his other birthdays and the crazy things that had happened at them. Ethan was especially interested in their stories, because he hadn't attended many of them. He hadn't known that there were other gifted at the past birthdays.

Max sat there smiling and laughing as they talked about the time Max smashed the Piñata before anyone arrived so he could get the candy he liked. He explained that he was too slow when swinging the stick and it never broke, so he fixed that problem. Another funny time, Jeremy was giving Max a horseback ride and Jeremy bucked Max too hard and he fell into the cake. Some thought that Jeremy did that on purpose, so he wouldn't have to eat the bland cake that they made for Max every year. Jeremy was grounded for a month and he ate the cake happily every year since then - and NO horseback rides before the party.

They continued with their own birthday stories, including Ethan's last birthday when Jeremy almost burned Ethan's hair off. He had tried to keep the candles from going out with magic but instead, they flared up. Ethan had been leaning over the cake, waiting to blow them out, and received a face full of fire. Only Atticus' quick thinking had prevented a disaster. The indoor storm soaked the cake, the guests and the dining room. Jeremy was grounded after that, too.

They chatted and laughed, teasing Jeremy the most for his bad luck. When they heard the doorbell ring again, Max was off like a frog.

PART TWO

MAX'S BIRTHDAY PARTY

Nearly fifty people arrived for the party over the next few hours. Max knew almost all of them and the ones he didn't remember reminded him who they were.

The beautiful Savannah brick clad, semi-detached, three story row house had balloons dressing the railings coming up to the front door. There was a silver banner announcing Max's Birthday. Once inside the remodeled house there were plenty of candles lit up around the rooms and more balloons decorating every space, including the open stairs leading to the next level.

The only room without balloons or decorations was the circle room. Not literally circular, the name came from the rituals performed there. Senona also stored and displayed most of her ritual antiquities there.

Oddly, nothing in the room was visible from the hallway. She used a reflecting spell that would direct interest away from the room. Anyone not part of her inner circle would see only what they thought was in the room and have no desire to enter.

Music livened the air. Max, Jeremy and Senona developed a play list everyone would enjoy. It included songs from Trout Fishing in America, classic rock, world music with a heavy Spanish and Latino section and some Top 10 popular songs. The music was almost drowned out by the children's chattering, the adults' conversation and the barking of Spartan as he was teased by the guests.

There was no shortage of food and PUNCH! Senona would prepare a different punch for each special occasion. Some of the guests would try to guess what punch she was going to make by what fruits were in season and who was the guest of honor. Very few had ever guessed correctly, but those who came close earned bragging rights. In fact, everyone loved her punch no matter what it had in it and always wanted the recipe. She would gladly share it, but no one ever quite enjoyed it as much when they made it themselves.

A few people knew the secret ingredient Senona and six centuries of witches added to the punch to make it special. Water for the ice was cleansed by the energy of a rose quartz before it was frozen and added to the punch.

The food brought by the witches was always amazing and they always brought food whether asked or not. Frog legs, goat heads and cow tongues were not on the menu, contrary to fairy tale recipes. The witches laughed at those stories. Instead, their clever use of quality ingredients and unique presentation of their signature dishes and desserts created the real magic. To create a food dish with magic only was considered a sacrilege to the goddess; only meals prepared with heart and hands blessed the recipient.

Food flooded tables and counter tops and plates were in everyone's hands. Max had his favorites and it wasn't hard to tell which foods they were. The rules were, "if you eat what we tell you all year long then on your birthday you can have whatever you want all day." Max's plate- actually plates- were full.

Max had his routine as always; he started with Ms. Sharon's spicy meatballs, he would open the crock pot and stick one meatball with a tooth pick and in two bites it was gone. He would then have one of the adults scoop up four or five onto a plate for him. On the same plate he would place a small piece of Ms. Christy's lasagna topping it with fresh Parmesan cheese. He would add a piece of French bread and a few tortilla chips.

Placing that aside, Max went straight for the table with Mr. Danny's Red Velvet Strawberry Delight cake, topped with fresh whipped cream. It was the lightest and sweetest angel food cake on earth. Max knew that everyone loved this dessert so he would always take two pieces just in case he wanted another piece later. To wash all this food down, Max had the largest cup he could find filled with his mom's punch.

This year's punch was Roberto's Bam Punch (lemon lime soda, orange juice, some frozen juice, a splash of grenadine and a splash of club soda). His mom liked to name her punches after people that inspired the idea for the punch, or simply someone who would be amused by it. These guests knew Max's favorites and that he had to be careful with what he ate, so they would moderate their recipes for him. They also knew where Max liked to hide his secret second plate, so they would occasionally go and add just a little more of one dish or take away a bit of another, to not upset his diet too much.

Over an hour into the party, the children were talking about school, new video games, clothes, books, movies and such. Some of the parents had nothing in common but their child and the weather, and so were talking about the St. Patrick's Day parade and if the weather this year was going to be warmer than the past few years. Luis was talking with a couple whose son went to school with Max.

"We don't bother going to the parade or festivities anymore," the wife stated. "The weather, the new rules the city has implemented, the crowds –it's just not worth the hassle. Doesn't all that Irish hoopla bother you, so close to your house?"

Luis answered, "We have been setting up a tent at 6am and dining in Chippewa square since before Jeremy was born. When I started my own business I gave all my employees the day off with pay. If they want, they too can eat, drink and celebrate in the square and watch the parade with us.

"Cultural festivities and beliefs are important to all of our stories, and I am sure that somewhere in my family tree I have a leprechaun. Savannah has the second largest St. Patrick's Day celebration in the country. With the number of clans still living among us, for one day we should all be Irish."

"I guess you give them Cinco de Mayo off to celebrate Mexico's Independence Day," the husband said.

Luis smiled. "Actually, Cinco de Mayo is not Mexico's Independence Day. That is September 16th. Cinco de Mayo commemorates the Mexican army's surprising victory over the French at the Battle of Puebla in1862." He laughed, "Although I am not from Mexico, I know that was a reason to celebrate. There are no true Spanish holidays that we celebrate here in the United States.

"I am actually from Valencia, Spain. It, too, is near the water, which is why I like Savannah so much. So where is it that you are from, my friends?" Luis asked his guests.

"We are from south Georgia, but I think my great grandfather was from Scotland or Wales somewhere like that," the wife replied.

"Then you may have some Irish in you after all," Luis observed.

Max had wandered into the family room and was watching a friend of Jeremy's playing a video game. The boy was very agitated and didn't want anyone to bother him. He was trying to get through a cavern with flames shooting up through the floor and poisonous snakes hanging from the ceiling.

When he yelled at Gretchen for disturbing him, Max turned off the T.V. and walked away. Jeremy quickly used some magic to turn the batteries around in the controller so it wouldn't work properly. Hearing the disturbance, Helen moved quickly toward the boy and gently touched his forehead, removing his negative energy. She then fell backwards onto the sofa, drained momentarily by his energy.

"Are you alright, Madame?" Camille asked.

"I will be," she replied. "That game really had a hold on him."

"Do you think he could be a Mirror Man?" Camille whispered in her ear, as some of the children of the others listened in.

"No, I don't think so. He was just very involved in that game. He did get very worked up over it for such a quiet little guy, didn't he?" Ethan's mom replied.

Using her telepathic skills, she asked Ethan to keep an eye on Jeremy's friend, who slouched in a chair in the corner. Gretchen was holding Max's hand when his mom announced it was time to sing Happy Birthday, eat cake and open presents.

Everyone piled into the family room as one of the guests pulled out his guitar and started to play a verse of Happy Birthday.

"Ok, we are now going to all sing to my baby Max, Happy Birthday!" Senora announced as the guitar player finished the first verse.

"Happy Birthday to youuuu, happy birthday to youuuu..." they seemed to get louder with each line. "Happy Birthday to Max, Happy Birthday to youuuuu!" From behind some adults a couple of voices rang out, "You look like a monkey and you act like one too!"

Senona didn't have to look far; it was Jeremy and Ethan. Senona shook her head, but Max was laughing so she held her tongue.

Max bent over the cake and with one big puff, blew all the candles out.

"What did you wish for?" someone asked.

Gretchen was still standing beside him and squeezed his hand. "If he told us, then it wouldn't be a wish anymore, would it?"

Gretchen looked at her father, who smiled and winked in her direction in support.

Max's father brought out a huge knife and handed it to Max to cut the first slice of cake. This had been their tradition since for long time, he explained to some concerned parents. Max didn't really like to eat decorated cakes, but he did like to look at them. He studied the cake and smiled. He liked the cake a lot, and there were no finger marks this year. He thought it through then cut a little corner of the cake so as not to ruin the soccer field that had been air-brushed on the top.

'HAPPY BIRTHDAY (Mr. Soccer) MAX', the cake read. Max really enjoyed playing and watched soccer; it was all he did if he was by himself in the court yard. Senona could see that Luis was biting his tongue. He would have preferred that it read Futbol, like in the rest of the world. But he understood the term soccer was used in North America, and after the debate at Jeremy's 7th birthday party that he had with a college football fanatical father he was told not to bring that up for discussion again.

Jeremy yelled, "My brother can juggle a ball on his foot and knee 30 times. He also scored two goals for his team last week. Watch out, Ethan - he will be better than you and Camille soon!" Jeremy was proud of his little brother's enthusiasm for soccer, even though he was more of a baseball guy himself.

"Sounds like I should be happy that he is not in my division," Ethan replied, smiling at Max.

Jeremy looked around for Camille, expecting her to say something too, but couldn't find her in the room. "Look Max, your mad soccer skills have already scared off Camille!" Jeremy said. Everyone started laughing.

Senona spoke up. "Excuse me friends, my husband and sons would like to thank all of you for coming to Max's birthday party. It is always a pleasure to meet our children's friends and their parents. We have one more tradition in our house and that is to open presents while you eat birthday cake. Then, as is custom, we will break the Piñata which will break up this celebration!"

Gretchen and Helen helped with handing Max birthday presents and with writing down who gave each gift to him. After opening half of the gifts and cards, Max asked if he could come back in a few minutes. As he walked away, Helen presumed that he must have to go to the bathroom. Max was hard to read and she tried not to get into the children's heads anymore than she needed too. She was a strong believer that they needed their privacy, too.

Some of the children were eyeing the Piñata, discussing how and where they were going to hit it for it to explode open. Others were happily eating birthday cake and looking a little sleepy. Max wanted some cake too, but he wanted Mr. Danny's Red Velvet Strawberry Delight. He had hidden a piece earlier in the circle room, behind the huge chair that his dad usually sat in.

As he turned the corner into the hall, he noticed that the door was open, just a bit. Wondering if had not closed it completely or if someone was in there, he slowed down. Someone was in the circle room! He heard pages of a book being turned and he saw a candle flickering. He really wanted his special cake and didn't want the intruder to get it either. Boldly, he took a few more steps. Pausing again, he saw the candle light go out and a little mouse run out through the crack of the door.

Max exhaled deeply, relieved but also perplexed and worried. Why would a mouse need a candle? Did it eat his Strawberry Delight? How did it get the door open?

First, he turned the lamp on next to the

chair and checked that his food was alright. Good. The little mouse didn't eat his cake. He climbed into his dad's chair to eat some of it, in case the mouse came back.

"Ahh," he sighed, then looked around the room to see if anything was different. He noticed that the panel on the cabinet with his mom's chalice and wand was open. He knew it wasn't like that before. He would have noticed it and closed it for her. He finished his cake and jumped down, placing the plate on the chair. He walked to the cabinet and looked in. The book was open on the shelf but nothing was missing, so he closed the book and replaced it with the others. As he did so, he took a deep breath. Oddly, he thought he smelled the lotion that Camille loved to wear.

As he was turning off the lamp, Camille opened the door wide. "So this where you are hiding! Everyone is waiting for you to come back and open the rest of your presents," she smiled and stared into his eyes. "Oh, don't worry. I won't tell them about the Strawberry Delight cake you were hiding; it is our little secret!"

Camille held the door open and held his hand all the way back to the table, where

Gretchen was still waiting to finish unwrapping the presents.

"I found him," Camille announced.

"Good!" Gretchen exclaimed. "I thought we were going to have a smack down if these BOYS don't get to hit that Piñata soon."

"Oh really, us boys you say Gretchen? I think it was you that broke the bat last year. You hit the fire place so hard you chipped the bricks!" Jeremy reminded her.

Max continued to open his gifts. Every gift Max opened was the best gift of all. He thanked everyone for everything and truly did like every toy and clothing item and book he received.

Helen saw Camille, Gretchen and a few other women cleaning up the paper and collecting the cards. "I will take care of cleaning up, ladies; you go watch the foolishness of the Piñata," Helen told them as she started picking things up.

As Camille started to walk away, Helen brushed her hand through her hair. "Is everything alright, my dear?" Helen asked.

"You have seemed a little off today. I know your father wishes that he were home more for you."

"No, it is not that Madame. I just have a lot of school work right now and soccer semi-finals are soon. Plus, I am a little nervous about playing the piano at one of the St. Patrick's Day events my father is hosting for the Grand Marshal. That's only a few weeks away," Camille replied a little nervously.

"Oh my, you do have a very busy schedule. I know your Mystic training is draining, too. I can see why you seem a little distracted. Have you thought about cutting anything out?" Helen asked, a little concerned that Camille was over-committed.

"No, there is nothing that I could cut out. I enjoy doing all of it. It will slow down soon, after St. Patrick's Day and soccer season," Camille assured her.

Hugging her tightly, Helen reminded her that if she ever needed a woman to talk to about anything, she would be there to listen.

"Thank you Madame," Camille replied as Helen released her from her embrace. "Ethan is very lucky to have such a great mother whose there for him, even though his father is out tracking down people who want to hurt us."

"We all love you Camille, and your father

and mother love you so very much. I know it must be hard not being allowed to see your mother, but I can assure you she is never far from you in her thoughts and with her love." Helen chose her words carefully when she spoke of Sophia. "Everything she did was for you and your father. I know you are old enough to understand that."

"Yes, of course Madame, I understand. It still doesn't make it any easier, though," Camille replied, a single tear rolling down her pale cheek.

Helen could sense that there was so much more going on inside poor Camille's head and body. She knew then that Gregory was right to be concerned. Camille was going through many different changes and emotions.

"Oh this is silly of me Madame. I am so sorry. I know that all this will pass soon. You must be worried and lonely without your husband around to help you with Ethan's training." Camille said as she wiped the tear from her cheek.

Helen wasn't sure what had just happened between the two of them. She wasn't used to young women and their spontaneous emotional breakdowns. She reassured Camille that she and Ethan were managing and that all the help the rest of the community was providing was invaluable.

"There is one thing," Camille said.

"I have been having these dreams with Mercy in them. We are fighting back to back, but I can't see what, and then I wake up."

Helen hadn't heard Camille's half-sister Mercy's name used in a while.

"That could mean the two of you are still well connected and are fighting for the same cause," Helen suggested, thinking that Mercy hadn't been seen or heard from in years. She was nothing like Camille and imagining them fighting as allies was difficult.

"I thought that, too," Camille agreed.

The laughter and groans were getting louder in the room with the Piñata. Camille took Helen's hand and kissed it. She smiled back and led her into the chaos of the beating of the Piñata.

"This is it! This time I am going to blow that thing open!" With those final words Ethan finished off the poor beaten, unrecognizable Piñata. Candy and toys flew all over the place and the children scurried to lay claim to their bounty.

"Ethan is going to be a good warrior and leader someday, as it has been written,"

Camille said, squeezing Helen's hand. "We are all going to be alright, in the end."

Helen looked at Ethan and then down at Camille, and for a moment wasn't sure who was the adult. She had been comforting Camille only minutes ago and now Camille seemed to have turned the tables. Helen smiled at Camille and put her arm around her.

"The gods and goddess have truly blessed all of us. Whatever they need of us, I know we will achieve through the best of our abilities," Helen replied.

Shortly after the breaking of the Piñata, people began to leave. They thanked Senona and wished Max a very Happy Birthday and a good year. Senona encouraged her guests to take food, but everyone was full, happy and tired. The women helped Senona clean up and the men who were left helped Luis move furniture back to its regular place. The children that were still left checked out some of Max's presents and ate some of the candy that they collected from the massive explosion of the Piñata.

"What were you doing most of the afternoon?" Jeremy asked Camille. "I saw you come in with Ethan and Gretchen and we hung out for a while, but then you disappeared."

"Are you my babysitter or something?" Camille snapped. "If it were any of your business, I was around, talking to people, doing stuff. I found Max didn't I? And I talked to Ethan's mom for a while. I am quite capable of existing without a babysitter friend."

"Alright, don't go all puberty on me," he replied, trying to laugh it off. He knew that she could out-talk him and somehow or another make him look like the bad guy. "Cool! I get it."

Jeremy then slapped Max on the back and said "Great party, little bro! I think this year went off without a hitch. How does it feel being another year older?"

Max was staring at Camille, then turned and looked at Jeremy and said, "I don't feel any different but I like being 8 years old now."

"Well I think you are a very great 8-year-old," Camille added. Max smiled at her, but something still seemed to be disturbing him.

"I think we have all had way too much junk food and are going to pay for it tomorrow," Gretchen laughed. "What was up with that kid playing that video game, Jeremy? I thought he was going to really kill someone if he didn't stop playing. After Ethan's mom got some kind of energy spike from him, I thought for a minute that maybe he was a Mirror Man."

"I guess we need to be a little more careful who we invite to everything from now on," Ethan said thoughtfully. "Probably our parents checked them out before they came, though."

"I can't wait till St. Patrick's Day weekend," Camille interjected.

"There is still one last birthday tradition from my family," Ethan said, looking at Max. "A pinch to grow an inch..."

Ethan and Jeremy chased after Max to give him his eight inches for the year.

CHAPTER SEVEN

THE SERENITY CHANNEL

Serenity: a quality or state of being serene; calm, still, peace, tranquility. Not words usually found in children's vocabulary between the ages of 10 to 15.

Channel: a path, stream; also, a fixed or official course of communication, or a direction of thought or information. Another word uncommonly used by young people.

The Serenity Channel was just that - a place of calm, simple and safe communication. No one remembers exactly when the Serenity Channel was started, or by whom. Rumors say that a young wizard created it to be able to commune with a young lady that was not of noble descent. Others insist a group of wood fairies used it to visit with young witches and still others say that it was brought by visitors from a distant planet, after they were given safe haven and assistance returning home. Whatever the truth, it now provided a place for the younger children to learn patience and centering skills.

Every child loved going to the Serenity Channel. There, they could talk freely with one another and learn new gifts and perfect others. After coming of age, entry was closed. This limitation was added in the late 1800s, to allow the children of the others a safe place to commune. Away from adult interference, they could start to develop their social skills and acceptance of one another's differences. Many parents reminded their children that this was their favorite part of growing up and still missed visiting.

Only one elder of each Sect, House and Clan was permitted in, merely to oversee the Serenity Channel happenings. They could remove a child if they were to overstep the laws of the Channel. The children rarely got out of hand while in the Serenity Channel, though. Why would they? They had the freedom to go anywhere and do just about anything to help them to grow and develop.

Most of the children liked to start their Serenity Channel journey in the comfort of their bedrooms or special place. Between gymnastics, dance classes, soccer games, swimming practices, martial arts, piano, guitar and vocal lessons most days of the week were pretty busy, except Mondays. Monday was the day that everyone had free time after school and loved going to the Serenity Channel.

Ethan went to the kitchen and poured a glass of water like he did every night, then squeezed two drops of lime into the water and went to his room. He wasn't sure what the lime was for, but it was what his parents did every night when they gave him water. He didn't really care much for it any other way, although he still puzzled over his parents' strict menu for him.

He stopped for a moment at the bathroom to brush his teeth quickly, and to rinse his face. He wasn't a big fan of teeth brushing, but he had never had a cavity in his young 10 years. Besides, if didn't brush them now his mother would have him do it before he went to sleep and that would be a bigger hassle. There is nothing worse than having to anything constructive when you are half asleep.

He knocked on his mother's bedroom door and told her that he was going to be chilling in his room until it was time for bed and that he had already brushed his teeth. Looking at him fondly, she got up out of the chair where she had been reading to give him a hug and kiss good night. Ethan returned the gesture and made his way to his room.

Ethan rested his head on his favorite pillow and read some of his journal entries from the past week. He found that this helped him concentrate as he worked on focusing his energy into the Serenity Channel. It still took him a little longer than most of the others, but he had always made it in. He just had to concentrate on his goal. His goal was always the same - to meet up with his friends. So he would concentrate on them, and as they reached out to him in their thoughts they eventually were together.

After only 15 minutes, Ethan was in. He looked around and saw that he was in an alley in an old city he did not recognize. He walked out of the alley and around the corner, where he saw Camille, Jeremy, Gretchen and a few other others. They were sitting on the front steps of a historic house on the other side of a city square. Oh, the city parks were one of many things that Ethan liked about visiting Jeremy. Even though he was at Jeremy's house for Max's birthday, they had stayed inside the whole time.

It wasn't that he didn't like living in the country with the acres of forest to play in, horses to ride and wild animals to chase. But the city always had something going on and the parks (or squares) were always bustling with tourists, young lovers and street artists. Ethan knew where he was now; he had passed this house and this park probably a hundred times in the car with his parents on the way to Jeremy's house. He waved at his friends; they stood up and waved back as he made his way over to them.

"Hey, this is cool place to meet this time," Ethan said, a little out of breath from his run across the park.

"It was Camille's idea, somewhere different from the regular places," Gretchen replied. They all liked going to famous places and would pick one ahead of time. Or they would go to Camille's back yard, where there was a pool, a fountain, and a maze in the garden that her father and mother had specially designed for them.

"I thought since we were all hanging out at Jeremy's a lot over the next few months, we should do a little investigation of the area and talk about things in the city. After all, we are getting a little older and I hope that our parents will let us have some freedom this year during St. Patrick's Day," Camille commented.

"I guess they will let us have a little space, but I can't imagine that they will allow us too much. I mean since there is still the threat of the Mirror Men out there," Jeremy said, looking at Camille as if there was something she wasn't telling them.

"I haven't felt or heard anything about them around here or even in this country since Beltane last year. I know that we are still tracking them; I hear my father speak of them on occasion, but no one has said anything either," Camille observed. She looked at them, and didn't say another word. After all who was going to argue with her when she was the oldest and could see the future?

"Come on, I know this area better than all of you. I will show you some pretty cool and funny things," Jeremy said, jumping up.

"Let's walk the St. Patrick's Day parade route," Camille suggested. "Do you know by heart?" she taunted him.

"Yeah, of course, I know the parade route, but I, I mean we can't walk the whole route tonight," he replied. Ethan and Gretchen looked at them, wondering what was on Camille's mind.

"Jeremy is right; it is a long route Camille," Gretchen added in Jeremy's defense.

Camille stood there looking around the park and the neighborhood as if she was searching for something specific. It was easy for them to tell when Camille was deep in thought. She had a tell, just like a poker player would with a good or a bad hand of cards. Camille would start to twirl her hair in her fingers when she was agitated.

"What's on your mind, Camille?" Ethan asked, after they had all watched her staring around the area for few minutes, twirling her hair the whole time.

"Just thinking of a dream I had about a bunch of lions guarding a man in a forest," she answered. "As a matter of fact, this area sort of looks likes the forest."

"This is definitely not a forest," Ethan replied. "You must be confused."

"I am never-" Camille started angrily.

"We can walk part of the parade route on this side of Savannah tonight and if you still want to walk the rest of it we can agree to meet on Bay Street under the row of live oak trees next time we come into the Serenity Channel," Jeremy interrupted, hoping to distract her.

"Ok Jeremy, I can live with that. Let's just start walking and talking. I mean, if you can do more than one thing at a time!" Camille teased, forgetting Ethan.

Jeremy shrugged his shoulders and replied, "If we walk down Bull Street towards the river, then turn on Liberty, then toward the river again on Abercorn, we will be almost at the beginning of the parade route and in front of Colonial Cemetery."

Everyone knew what he meant but his directions did not seem clear at all. "Unless you are all afraid of a few ghosts walking around?" he added, elbowing Ethan while looking at Gretchen.

"Ha, ha, very funny," Gretchen replied. "They are not the same as me to start with, both because they are very dead and really not happy, too."

As they walked they talked about what was

happening at school, soccer, music lessons and about their other friends and family. Since no one else could see them unless they too were in the Serenity Channel, they could check out what people were watching on television and get dogs to bark for no real reason. It was all just fun and a way to get to know each other a little better.

"So what did you mean about the ghosts being very dead and really unhappy too, at the Old Cemetery?" Ethan asked Gretchen.

"Well, it is the Old Colonial Cemetery to start with. They have to lock it up at night because people like to mess around in there and cause damage and stuff. That gets the city commission upset and the people laid to rest there get upset too," Gretchen explained. "So the story goes, when the city was expanding Abercorn Street they started digging up the road and well they were digging up caskets and bodies, too. So rather than have to move even more bodies, they decided to pave right over them."

"No way, that is nuts! How could they do that?" Ethan exclaimed quietly.

"That isn't even the best story," Camille added. "The real reason for all the chaos and why Gretchen gets upset is because they over crowded the cemetery for over a hundred years."

Ethan looked, perplexed, at Camille. "I don't get it. What do you mean overcrowded and how is that a bad thing? I mean people have been burying people on top of each other for thousands of years," Ethan said curiously.

They sat down on a brick stair case leading up to a beautiful front door with green lights framing it.

"I know you have heard all kinds of stories about how haunted, magical and mystical Savannah really is, right?" Camille started.

Pausing to collect her thoughts, she absentmindedly began to twirl her hair. "Colonial Cemetery was the only registered cemetery in Savannah for over a hundred years (1750-1853). Nearly everyone who died in Savannah during this time was buried there and they weren't all happy about it. More than nine thousand bodies are buried in only six acres.

Some families with burials in Colonial Park - that's what they called it back then - moved the remains of their loved ones to new cemeteries outside of Savannah. As unhappy as many residents of Savannah were about the overcrowding, just as many dead in the cemetery weren't interested in moving, so their spirits still lingered.

"Many residents of Savannah were upset with the Park and Tree Commission when they began to organize the park in 1896. They felt that the grave markers placed by the Georgia Historical Commission were inadequate because they only discussed the fancy pants in the cemetery and not lesser known Savannahians."

Camille stopped talking when an orange tabby cat leapt into her arms. Another strange thing about the Serenity Channel was that only certain animals could have contact with both worlds, and the cat of course was one of them.

"So I guess that there are still a lot of lingering spirits in and around the cemetery. But isn't that the same in most cemeteries?" Ethan commented as Camille stroked the head of the cat.

Jeremy decided that this was a perfect opportunity to add his stories about the Colonial Cemetery. "Yeah, but they don't all have Archibald Bulloch the first President of Georgia before it was a state; Major General Nathaniel Greene; James Habersham, Royal Governor of the Georgia back in 1771 and his son Joseph Habersham, Postmaster General under three Presidents; Lachlan McIntosh, Major General, Continental Army; Samuel Elbert, Revolutionary soldier and Governor of Georgia; Capt. Denis L. Cottineau de Kerloguen who aided John Paul Jones in the engagement between the "Bon Homme Richard" and the "Serapis"; and Hugh McCall, early historian of Georgia. There are plenty of others too but these are my favorite ones," Jeremy explained.

"Aren't you forgetting a few other facts, Jeremy?" Gretchen added. "Like the fact that there were many shooting victims from duels that were held just behind the cemetery in what is now a playground. Button Gwinnett was killed there in a duel with rival Lachlan McIntosh. There is also a mass grave dug behind the cemetery in 1820 for the dead from the city's worst fire on record. Nearly 500 buildings were destroyed while many residents slept. Many of them still don't even know they are dead, and are walking around looking for their families.

"That same year over 600 people died of a yellow fever epidemic and many of them were buried in that same mass grave," Gretchen added passionately.

They got up from the porch and continued walking quietly down Liberty Street, which marked the outskirts of the settlement of Savannah in the early 1800's. When they did continue to talk, it was about what it might have been like if they were kids back then. They quickly decided they were happy that they were not.

"You could probably ask your father what it was like back then," Camille said, looking in Ethan's direction. "I have heard him talk with some of the elders about his excursions up and down the inter-coastal waterways between Boston, New York, Savannah and Charleston. As a matter of fact, I heard your father has put a few people in that cemetery for stealing from his business!" Camille added.

Ethan didn't know how to respond to her. First, his father had not ever discussed his past with him. Second, because he was trying to do the math in his head to figure out how old his father be to have been alive back then and third, he hoped that that if the spirits were still there, they wouldn't think he resembled his father and get mad at him.

"Well, if his father did put some of them in there, than they probably deserved it," Jeremy decided.

"Let's face it; Savannah has always been a wonderful but weird kind of city," he continued, more comfortable with his history lesson than talk of restless spirits. "General James Oglethorpe landed here in 1733 with 120 diverse passengers and named the 13th and final American colony 'Georgia' after England's King George II. Savannah was Georgia's first city and Oglethorpe welcomed everyone to the new city. My father told me that they were free to worship as they pleased; just no lawyers, no rum and no slavery. Oglethorpe even became friends with the local Indian chief Tomochichi so they never had any real fights like other colonies.

"Savannah survived many battles with the English and French over the years. Then Union General William Tecumseh Sherman marched into Savannah after burning Atlanta and everything else in his path during the Civil War. He spared Savannah, saying it was one of the most beautiful places he had seen. He gave Savannah to Abraham Lincoln as a Christmas gift in 1864," Jeremy informed them.

"You know, Jeremy if you could remember all this in school then you would have an

A in social studies," Camille commented sarcastically.

"I think if they taught us like this in school we would probably remember the history since we would know the stories," Ethan suggested.

The Serenity Channel had a way of teaching the children as they enjoyed time together. No one knew the magic involved but somehow the actions and conversations of the children developed into constructive learning exercises, whether they realized it or not. This was another reason why parents didn't mind the children spending time in the Serenity Channel and why they wished they could return.

Just steps away from the Colonial Park Cemetery, Gretchen began to feel uneasy butterflies in her stomach. Of all of the children, she most sensed everything still happening at the park. She could see and feel the spirits as they moved around, some aimlessly, while others clearly on missions. One of them had been lingering in the shadows since they turned off of Liberty Street.

"Oh yuck," Camille commented, and then explained to the boys that two young lover ghosts were kissing under an oak tree.

"Cool, which oak tree?" Jeremy asked as he tried to tune into the young lovers.

"Really... Jeremy! If you can't see them than I am not going to point them out to you," Camille replied.

Ethan looked around and thought he could hear their voices but was having a hard time seeing their figures. The more he focused on the sounds, he could begin to make out voices but still only saw light and shadows.

"What's the matter Ethan?" Gretchen asked.

"Nothing really, but ..." he stuttered.

"You can't see them that well, can you?" Camille observed.

"I can hear most of what's going on but I cannot see much more than shadows and blurry light moving around," Ethan admitted reluctantly.

"That is pretty normal for vampires," Camille replied.

"Then why can I see Gretchen when she goes all ghost-like?" Ethan protested.

"Can you really see her or is it just her energy that you feel?" Camille asked.

As he stood there looking around, thinking about Camille's question, he heard a gunshot and ducked.

"Cool, they are going to have a duel tonight," Jeremy shouted to the others.

"Arrr! You wretched children disappoint me, mates!" The voice came from behind them.

"Who? What is that?" Ethan responded nervously.

"Aye bin listen to you's children as you talks about thee histories of this here port of Savannah. You's disappointed me's in your memories of who thee real stories 'bout, mates!" the voice said as a figure slowly showed itself from the shadows. "Ha,ha, ha! You's children forget about me!"

"Is he a pirate?" Ethan asked cautiously. "He sounds like a pirate, and kind of smells like what I think a pirate would smell like."

"Yes, he is a pirate!" Jeremy and Gretchen replied in unison.

"I hadn't forgotten about the pirates and your importance in the history of Savannah. But we were talking about the history of Colonial Cemetery, sir," Jeremy explained hastily to the irritated pirate.

"Aye, but they be pirates buried 'ere too, lad," the pirate replied. "Ye tinks thee fancies of dis 'ere town is goings to note dis. Me mates an' me's brings thee barrows on shore through thee tunnels. If ye drop in de tunnels, we move dem here, lad."

"So what does that have to do with Colonial Cemetery?" Jeremy asked, not really clear on pirate language.

The pirate looked at him angrily, and Ethan hurriedly piped in.

"I think what he is saying is that he was one of the crew on a regular ship that came to port in Savannah a few times a year. He would be in charge of moving liquor, weapons and people in and out of the city through secret tunnels to the river. If someone died or was killed in the tunnel, he was the one that would sneak them to the back of the cemetery through a tunnel and bury them with the other bodies," Ethan explained.

"Dat's what I been saying," the pirate barked. "I know's that you be as smart as you's pop's der lad! I see's it in those eye's of you's." The pirate reached out and touched Ethan's face.

"Hey, what was that?" Ethan yelped. He couldn't really see but felt the dry cracked boney fingers of the pirate touching his cheek.

"Not so cold as you's pop's but surely as strong as he," the pirate decided.

"See, I told you that your father had been back and forth from Savannah for a few hundred years," Camille exclaimed.

"No, you said that he might have put a few bodies in the cemetery," Gretchen corrected.

"Aye, de lad's pop's did help some of thee residents find der way here. Some of dem he killed to live, others he killed to save," the pirate spirit added mysteriously, a twitchy grin on his face only the girls could see.

The four children looked at each other for a few minutes, not wanting understand everything that the pirate was saying. They understood that Atticus was an old vampire that looked really good for his age, and that he had to feed to survive. They knew the good that he did for people and wanted to believe the good outweighed the bad. They were reminded that Ethan would have to do the same someday. For now, though, he was just their best friend.

"I am sure that whatever our friend's father did back them he did because he had to survive," Camille replied. "I would like to know more about the secret tunnels under the city. Are they still there?" she added. She hoped changing the subject to secret tunnels would take everyone's mind off of this wretched pirates' rant about Atticus. What pirate wouldn't like to brag about knowing a secret, she thought cleverly.

"Most of dem are still here's me lady, yes! I could tells you about's dem if aye gots a few hours," the pirate offered.

A few of the spirits were starting to fight just outside the iron fence that was supposed to keep them in and the living out. One of them made a gesture toward Gretchen and another one turned to stare at her.

"I think we should start back now," Gretchen suggested, tugging at Camille's sleeve.

"Yeah, maybe we should be leaving," Jeremy added, sensing Gretchen's concern.

"What? Is there something going on that I can't see?" Ethan asked, noticing their strained voices and awkward expressions.

"I believe we have worn out our welcome," Camille agreed. "I would still like to know about the tunnels, though. Would you like to walk a little with us sir?" she asked the pirate.

Without hesitation the pirate started away from the cemetery with them.

"What is your name?" Gretchen asked the pirate.

"Me name, me name," he thought out loud. "They call me Mutt, me's name is Mutt."

"Mutt? That is an odd name," Gretchen commented.

"Well, that be what they's call me!" the pirate answered defiantly.

"Can we call you Mutt too?" Gretchen asked, apologetic.

"Aye, dat would be fine," Mutt replied.

"My name is Gretchen; that is Jeremy and Camille. I guess you already know Ethan, Lord Atticus' son," Gretchen replied, pointing to each of the others as she told him their name.

"Tell us about the tunnels that are under Savannah!" Camille interrupted almost desperately. "Are they still open? Does anyone use them?"

"There be still a few of dem around and I 'ear tell dat they be used. There are two dat go to the river, one be at thee old pub, I thinks thee call it The Pirate's House. A fine name for a pub if ye not a pirate! The other be under the market where thee party be.

"Then ye got 4 or 5 or 3, aye maybe 6 that run through the city from parks to thee old buildings. Then ye got thee old cisterns dat follow the streets and parks that Old Oglethorpe had them build to keep the buggy routes from muddyin' up and washin' away.

They connect to thee tunnels, too," Mutt replied.

"That seems like a lot of tunnels for a city that is built at sea level!" Gretchen replied.

"Aye, that it is but they designed thee city to drain back to the sea, dis is why there is 3 levels to thee wate," Mutt replied confidently. "Ye come to thee port dock first, den you come to thee market place, then ye come up to thee city. Each level has tunnels, you see."

"I heard that not only did people get smuggled in and out of the city by the tunnels but many people used the tunnels to get back and forth between buildings to avoid being stoned or robbed," Camille stated.

"Aye, thee fancy pants that didn't like to share be what's you be speaking of my dear. They be likin' their drink and booty so as not to have to share wit' thee commoner," Mutt agreed.

As they came upon the next square, Camille stopped and stared, appearing surprised and terrified at the same time. Gretchen stopped and asked her if she was alright. Mutt and the boys stopped too and had turned around to walk back in her direction.

"This park, it looks familiar. Look - there are lions on pedestals and they look like they are guarding the statue guy. I was telling you earlier...my dream about a forest with a man being guarded by lions," Camille explained.

"Look at the park from here; doesn't it look like a forest with all the trees around it? Tell me that isn't a man being guarded by lions!"

"What are you talking about, Camille? We come to this park at least once a year. This is where my father sets up the tent for the St. Patrick's Day Parade," Jeremy replied, confused. "How could you not have recognized this park in your dream, Camille?"

She stood frozen, staring through Jeremy at the square.

"Aye this here park be Chippewa square, and that there man be Olde General James Oglethorpe," Mutt confirmed.

As they entered one of the walkways into the square, Ethan commented that he had counted 21 live oak trees and 6 palm trees, Jeremy replied that there were actually 23 live oak trees and 8 palm trees. Now that they thought about it, it did seem like a little forest to them, no matter how many trees there were exactly.

"I guess I hadn't really paid much attention to the statues or all the trees in the past,"

Camille said, bemused. "We are usually watching the parade, avoiding silly people or eating. When we are here on St. Patrick's Day, a lot more is going on."

Tonight there were only a few couples sitting on the benches, some kissing and others curled up like they were sleeping. They walked up to the foot of the statue where the lions sat. Camille studied them and laid her hands on them as if she were petting them. This would have seemed strange for anyone else, but given the relationship Camille had with cats this was pretty normal, even if they were solid stone.

"Are there tunnels under this park?" Camille asked Mutt as she continued to walk around the statue, studying its design and landscape.

"I tolds ya before that there be a cistern that run under these here parks, but a tunnel I don'ts know," Mutt replied, muttering. "There maybe's one or two I hear talk of, I don'ts know where they goes to. I don't needs to come dis a way too much."

"Is there something on your mind?" Gretchen asked Camille.

Smiling, Camille replied, "Maybe, maybe

not. I just have this feeling, like there's something I'm missing."

"Well, I am having this feeling that you are not telling us something. If you don't want to talk about it, fine," Gretchen replied.

Meanwhile Jeremy and Ethan were sitting on a bench, talking away with Mutt about all his adventures. Ethan wanted to ask him some questions about his father, but he didn't know if he wanted to hear the answers. In the end, he stayed away from questions all together. Mutt didn't need prompting to talk about the old days.

He told them about how he would take drunken men and woman to the ships through the tunnels and he would get paid in coin and drink for each one that he delivered unharmed. He told them about a bar maid that he fancied in Savannah. He would bring her perfumes and silks when he returned to port a few times a year. Mutt described his years on the seas as exciting and dangerous. They may have been pirates, but they were not the only threat on the seas.

After nearly an hour of Mutt telling them his tales, Camille and Gretchen interrupted them. They had been told to leave the Serenity

Channel and get a good night's sleep. The boys complained bitterly, but soon agreed.

"It was really good to meet you, Mutt," Ethan said.

"You were really a great help with understanding some more about the city from that time period. I promise to include the importance of the pirates in my stories about Savannah in the future!" Jeremy added.

Mutt grunted and gave a crooked smile. "Aye, don'ts forget me now and ye be careful when doin' foolish things."

They exchanged quick glances, thinking that they were always careful, especially when doing something dangerous.

"I had one last question for you," Jeremy said curiously.

"What be that?" Mutt huffed.

"How did you die and why haven't you moved on?" Jeremy asked carefully.

"Remember the woman I say that I bring da perfumes for? Well she did not tells me that she had her a husban'. He be the caretaker of Colonial Park Cemetery. One night I be givin' the woman a peck in thee tunnel before I leaves again. He comes up behind me and whacks me on my noggin' with a shovel. The next thing me know I be buried in a stone wall bein' built around the cemetery."

"You mean he buried you alive in the stone wall?" Ethan asked.

"Aye that he did mate, and me knew that was a'comin someday," Mutt nodded.

"So why didn't you move on after you died? You don't have family or friends here, and you know that you are dead," Jeremy insisted.

"Argh, he did worse than that mate, he took my sack of coins and purchased a bar o' his own. He made me lady work like an animal every night 'til she died too of worry bones," Mutt replied. "So now we haunts his guests and family generation to generation, till we scares them all to death," Mutt added proudly.

Nothing more needed saying after that. "Thanks again, until we hear and see you again," Ethan said politely to the slight disturbance in the air from where he had heard Mutt's voice.

"Aye, good night," Mutt replied cheerily as he disappeared into the night air.

The four of them wandered up Bull Street towards Jeremy's house. Camille walked backwards, watching the others. "You know this is the perfect city for us to blend into the landscape. The old history and the ghosts suit us.

I mean, look at us. A ghost girl, a witch/gargoyle boy, a vampire boy and a mystic seer/sorceress girl are walking together down 300 year old streets. Compare that to the pirates, witch doctors, ghosts, Indians and new settlers who once trod these cobblestones," Camille mused.

"What does that have to do with the haunted cemetery and you acting weird since we entered the Serenity Channel?" Gretchen persisted as they faded back into the physical realm.

CHAPTER EIGHT

GOALS AND DISTRACTIONS

"Camille take the shot, it is all you!" Jeremy cheered from the bleachers.

The soccer coach yelled, "Camille, the right side is open - put it in the net!"

Camille had been playing soccer for as long as she or anyone else could remember. She played every position on the field and was the highest scoring mid-fielder in the district. She handled the ball skillfully, had great intuition on the field and always displayed good sportsmanship. She even helped with a U-6 recreation league. Her idol was Mia Hamm, and she thought wistfully about receiving a soccer scholarship.

When Camille received the ball normally, it was going in the net or to a striker that was going to score. But today her thoughts were interrupting her concentration. She watched the net, hesitating and then looking again before kicking the ball.

"Agh," Jeremy yelled out as the goal keeper moved back into position to stop the ball as Camille kicked it. With only a minute left in the game, it looked like this was going to be their first loss of the season.

As the whistle blew to end the game, there was a loud sign from the crowd of nearly 200 students, parents and teachers that had come to watch the girls' undefeated team. Camille congratulated the other team on their win and walked back to the bench. The coach always, had a short game recap with them.

As she approached the bench one of the students shouted, "Hey number 5, you had an open net. Why didn't you take the shot a minute earlier?" She heard a parent comment that she had left work early today to see her daughter play for the first time and they lost. Camille heard them but knew that it was the coach's responsibility to discuss the game with the spectators.

She did think to herself that if they could run for 60 minutes nonstop than they should get out on the field. If that parent that had seen any of the first 8 games, in which she had scored or assisted on every goal and they won, she may not be so quick to judge.

"Sorry coach," Camille sighed as she sat down with the other players.

"We win as a team, and we lose as a team," the coach replied. "Today we had some chances, including that last one of yours, Camille, but we didn't capitalize. We let them have one early. We didn't give up but it just wasn't meant to be today, girls. Now bring it in and let these fans know that one loss can't break our spirit!"

"One! Two! Three! Bobcats!!!!" the girls chanted, then broke off to leave.

Camille followed her ritual after the game. She sat down on the bench and removed her cleats and shin guards before leaving the field. She put on some sandals to give her feet a break and not ruin her cleats on the asphalt. As she sat there, some of her team mates reassured her that she had played hard and she was not to blame for the loss. Camille smiled and thanked them for the kind words and reassured them that they would win the next game. They smiled back and told her that they weren't going to lose another game this season.

She stood and stretched her legs, picked

up her gear and walked in the direction of her father. She could see the big smile on his face. Coming to her soccer games was the best release that Gregory had from both his daily routine and his mystical commitments. He would cheer her and the team, making supportive comments like "keep the ball in front of you" or "mark up", as if he was helping.

Gregory was very proud of all Camille's accomplishments. He knew that if she didn't succeed at something she expected of herself, she would be harder on herself than he could ever be. He had thought that there may be something on her mind distracting her; he knew that when the time was right, she would talk with him about it.

As Camille made her way to in her father's direction the coach caught up with her and stopped her. "Camille," she said in her calm and soothing voice.

"Yes Coach, what is it?" Camille replied, sensing that the coach was going to make sure she was alright.

"Am I playing you too much or pushing too hard?" the coach asked. The girls' soccer coach was a very laid-back teacher. She had a passion for the sport, but also felt that it was her position to guide and inform the girls, not to push to win. She was very knowledgeable concerning the game, which Camille admired in her coaching strategy.

"Absolutely not, Coach! Things have just been a little crazy these past few weeks or so. I am sure that this, too, will pass," Camille answered. She glanced at her dad for confirmation.

"I feel that Camille is just a bit tired. I am sure that she will have a better game next time," Gregory replied confidently.

"Of course she will," Coach replied. "I never have any worries with Camille on the field or in class."

As the coach walked off, Jeremy came running up to them, followed closely by Luis.

"I can't believe you girls lost your first game. I mean you can't always expect to win but last time you blew three balls by that goal keeper," Jeremy exclaimed.

"I feel you were robbed on some off-side calls and some time," Luis added as he got closer.

"We still didn't score a goal and we lost 1-nil," Camille pointed out.

"Are they going to win the next game,

sir?" Jeremy asked, looking in Gregory's direction.

"You know that we don't use our gifts for such trivial things as a game, particularly when it involves family," Gregory chided.

"Maybe I can make a sleep serum and put it in the other teams' water cooler before the game," Jeremy suggested, impressed with himself.

"There is no question that you could do that, Jeremy, but that wouldn't be fair to the other team. Winning means being the better team when matched evenly," Gregory said, smiling at Jeremy and Luis.

"He certainly has good school spirit, even if it is a little wicked. Which I am sure he gets from his mother's side of the family," Luis commented and smiled at Gregory.

"Hey, do you want to go get some pizza with us boys?" Luis asked Camille and her father.

Looking at Camille, Gregory could see that she was not really interested in going anywhere but home. "I think we both have a few things to do still this evening, but we do appreciate the offer. Next time I am sure," Gregory replied, shaking Luis' huge hand. "Jeremy, don't you go trying to double up the bacon on that pizza pie and end up baking a pig!" Gregory added.

Luis laughed. Jeremy could easily make that mistake, being at that stage. "Good call, Gregory," Luis said laughing. "I suppose then that we will see you two at the St. Patrick's Day parade, if not before," he added.

"We wouldn't miss it," Camille assured him quickly.

"Yes, we will be there. As a matter of fact, my little girl will be playing a piano recital for the Grand Marshal tomorrow night!" Gregory announced with much pleasure in his voice.

"Excellent!" Luis replied. "I guess we are off for that loaded pizza now."

Gregory didn't intend to be a pesky father, but he needed to know what was distracting Camille so much. They drove for five minutes before the silence was broken.

"How many people do you think will be at the party for the Grand Marshal tomorrow night?" Camille asked.

"I believe that there were two hundred invitations sent out. Is that what has been distracting you, my dear?" he replied cautiously. Stage fright jitters were easily handled. He knew that she had performed for large audiences without issue in the past, but that was when her mother was still around.

"I haven't wanted to pry, but I have felt your distance and secrecy from me. I am concerned that, well..."

Camille stopped her father. She wasn't exactly sure what he was going to say next but she knew that she didn't really want to find out, especially if it was about the girl thing.

"There is a lot going on with me right now and I don't really want to talk about it with you. I don't mean this in a bad way, but I wish Mother was around," Camille explained softly, staring out the car window at the passing fence posts.

Gregory had anticipated this discussion and knew it could go one of two ways. He wanted to take control of its direction, but before he could say anything, Camille started to cry softly. She didn't often release her emotions and he recognized that something great was burdening her. Gregory pulled the car off to the side so he could reach over to hold his daughter as she expressed herself. They were always very careful not to read each other, as a sign of respect and understanding, so Gregory held her firmly but did not pry into her mind's eye.

"I miss her so much!" Camille cried into his chest. "I feel her with me all the time, but I miss her touch, the way she made everything just right, even the way you two cheered me on at soccer games together when I was still tripping over the ball."

Gregory sighed into her hair, remembering her mother Sofia. When Sofia and Gregory had met, it had been love at first site. She was a magnificently beautiful creature who Gregory thought he did not deserve, and yet she was overcome with love for him. They shared their lives only briefly. Before their journey together ended, Sofia gave birth to Camille and created their amazing family.

"I miss her every minute of every day, Camille. But I know that she is always with us and shares in our lives whether we are physically together or not." Gregory wiped the warm tears from Camille's cheeks.

"It's not fair. All the other children have perfect families, but ours had to be split up by some ancient rule from like, 2000 years ago," Camille protested.

"It could have been worse, my dear. They could have killed her. I did everything I could to plead with the elders to spare her from death so that she could at least feel your life as you grew," her father explained.

Silence fell heavily as they thought of Sofia, banished for eternity to an asylum. Neither had right words to continue and so Gregory buckled himself back in and continued their drive home. Not another word was uttered until they pulled into the garage and turned off the car.

"I am a good listener, Camille," he reminded her, grabbing her gear from the trunk. "But I do realize that there are things that are best to discuss with women. Ms. Helen and Ms. Senona are always available to talk with you, but I want us to always be able to talk about our family issues together," Gregory said, looking Camille in the eyes.

Camille dropped her school bag on the ground and hugged her father tightly around the waist. "I will try harder, Father," Camille sighed.

"I would like to go for a short swim to relax before dinner. Is that alright with you?" Camille asked.

The sun was going down quickly. Despite this, Gregory agreed, sensitive to her needs. He assured her that he would be out momentarily to keep an eye on her. Camille gave him a smile that melted his old heart and ran off to change.

When she returned, he headed to his office where he picked up a woven headpiece made from vines, flowers and leaves. He held it in his hands for a few minutes and whispered, "Our baby girl is growing up."

By the time Gregory returned to the pool, the light was fading and Camille was no longer swimming. He could feel her energy but she was nowhere to be seen. When he turned around as to walk into the house, he saw twenty fireflies dancing over the pool. He knew then that she was in her special place, a magical room that he and Sofia had secretly designed in the side of the pool. He should have known that she only wanted to go swimming this night so that she could commune with her mother. He had done the same with Sofia's old headpiece, still green and fragrant after the many years since she had last worn it.

Fifteen minutes passed and Camille stepped out of the pool. Awaiting her were several fairies holding up a large towel to warm her. Lilith curled around her legs and she picked her up and started to stroke her silky fur.

"I hope you enjoyed your swim." The voice came from a chair just outside the large glass doors leading into the kitchen area. "Dinner is waiting on you," her father said as he became clearer in the light.

"Yes, sir, thank you. I needed that," Camille replied, hurrying up the stairs and into the house.

CHAPTER NINE

PREPARATIONS

As the week before St. Patrick's Day shortened, everyone was trying to complete last minutes jobs, chores, and projects. Jeremy and Max were busy tracking down all of their green beads, green leis, shamrock glasses, 'Kiss me, I'm Irish Buttons', green and orange hair spray dye and so on. Even though they were not Irish themselves, their mother loved St. Patrick's Day. She had often told them it was a great time for everyone to get together and enjoy a fun festival before Beltane and the preparation of spring.

"Everyone is Irish on St. Patrick's Day," Jeremy reminded Max. "Did I tell you about the time that I went to school dressed like a little Irish man?" Jeremy asked.

"When I was in pre-school, Mom had

dressed me up for school parade on St. Patrick's Day. I remember it so well because some bigger kids laughed at me when I arrived with orange hair and a 'Kiss me I'm Irish' button for a school parade."

"Oh no, Jeremy that is very bad of them. I'm sorry!" Max exclaimed.

"Thanks Max, but it was ok, you will see," Jeremy replied, smiling at Max. "Someone yelled, 'Look at the little Spanish boy with the orange hair and funny button!' I didn't know what to think. One of the older boys came up to me and rubbed my head and took some of the hair dye onto his hands. I turned and bit him on the hand quickly, like a cat nipping a stranger for touching it while sleeping. Then I muttered three words – 'Hooligan, Hooligan, Freckles.' I remembered Mom using this chant once when a bully stole from our table at the parade." Jeremy stopped for a moment, collecting his thoughts.

"Did you get in trouble? Did the boy get hurt?" Max asked worriedly.

"That's just it Max. The teachers came running to deal with my behavior, but the boy had bright orange spots breaking out on his body, like over-sized freckles. That was pretty funny! Some people laughed, some sighed, but then Mom had to fill out a ton of paperwork for me biting. I still think she was not that mad, though, since I took care of the bully myself. It was also the last time the school had any incidents like that," Jeremy said.

"I am sorry, Jeremy. I guess they know everyone is Irish on St. Patrick's Day now, don't they?" Max added, laughing at the idea of this boy turning orange.

"Yeah, that's for sure!" Jeremy agreed.

"What's going on down here?" a voice called down the stairs. "Are you two ok?" It was their mom; she was familiar with those laughs and knew they were up to something.

"We're alright Mom, just laughing over a joke Max told me," Jeremy replied. He knew better than to bring up that story again. She would just get upset or worried and he did not want to deal with either.

"Ok," she replied, still hard at work putting together her own things for the big day. "Please don't forget that big box that your Uncle Philip sent us last month from Ireland," she added.

Staring at Max with a look of utter confusion, Jeremy answered, "I won't, Mom. We have it all under control."

Fortunately for Jeremy, Max remembered exactly where they had placed it when it had arrived in early February. Max had an amazing gift of remembering where things were last seen, what people said exactly and completing tasks down to the smallest detail.

"Good, it hasn't moved," Jeremy said as Max opened up the closet where it was stored. Max knew that Jeremy had forgotten that he had put it there but he wasn't going to say anything to his big brother.

"I wonder what Uncle Philip sent us this year?" Jeremy wondered out loud.

Uncle Philip O'Sullivan was some distant relation to their father Luis. He was probably one of the oldest relatives that they had, but he looked only around 35 years old. He swore it was because he did what he wanted, when he wanted and how he wanted. That is probably why most of the family refers to him as 'Blarney Phil O'Sullivan'.

A few years ago, he had come to the United States for St. Patrick's Day in Boston and got the entire city drunk for two days. Someone had told him that Irish beer was like river water and no one would drink it for enjoyment except on St. Patrick's Day. So he turned the entire city water supply into Irish beer and people couldn't stop drinking it. Fortunately for Boston, the O'Sullivan Clann had a curse placed upon them many years ago and their spells last only a short time. Three days of beer was more than enough, however.

There were more stories about his travels that had evolved into some big tales. Jeremy's favorite was when he couldn't find a suitable place to live; he rowed a boat out into a bay and speared the bottom with his Shillelagh walking stick. He said an island grew up out of the water with a huge blackwood tree right in the middle of it. He lived there for many years, until a group of investors wished to buy it for the tree so that they could carve amazing Shillelagh walking sticks and sell them as magical. Uncle Phil sold them the island and three months later the island started to sink along with the tree.

"I bet it is full of Claddagh bubble makers," Jeremy guessed.

"I bet it is full of pots of gold," Max said.

Standing in the doorway listening to them try and guess what was in Uncle Phil's box their mom added, "Well if it is pots of gold it would be fool's gold and if it's Claddagh bubble makers then the bubbles will probably explode when popped!"

She was all too familiar with the O'Sullivan sense of humor and some of the gifts that he had sent before reflected it. Once he sent a box full of packaged green tissues with an Irish prayer printed on the outside of them. They handed them out to parade guests and for three days everyone that used them for their noses had green noses and eyes. If they used them on their bottoms, well you know what was green, too. Another time, he sent plastic hats which after three hours melted onto people's heads and dyed their hair green. Senona was not going to trust him easily.

"What do you think is in it, Mom?" Max asked.

"By the size of the box (14" X 14") and the faint sent of peppermint, I am thinking that it is a box full of dirt-tasting mints!" she decided.

Both of the boys laughed at the thought of Uncle Phil sending a box full of dirt-tasting mints. Then their laughter stopped when their mom opened the box and found ten packages full of individually wrapped green mints with the Claddagh on each of them.

"Hey, I was close," Jeremy exclaimed when

he saw the Claddagh symbol of friendship and love on the packaging.

"Not bad, Jeremy," his mom replied while Max patted his brother on the arm. "So maybe you should try one of them to see if they really taste as good as they smell."

Jeremy hesitated as he looked at the box of green mints. He turned and looked up at his mother and back then at Max. How bad could it be? he thought, as one minute ticked by like an hour.

Out of nowhere a voice echoed, "I'll try one."

They turned around and to their surprise Uncle Phil was standing alongside their father in the hallway. He was dressed in green and grey from head to toe. Yes, he had his shiny black Shillelagh walking stick in one hand, pressing it over his shoulder like a sword.

"He gave me a call this morning from the airport and said that his hotel room had been double-booked," Luis explained as Senona started tapping her foot. "I told him that there would be NO relative of ours staying in a hotel while in our town. Let's make some room for Uncle Phil to stay here for a few days and show some of our Irish southern hospitality."

There was silence in the room; the boys knew not to say a thing until their mom did. She was still tapping her foot along with exhibiting an eyebrow twitch that was better known as the "we should have talked about it first" twitch.

"First things first," Senona stated. "Why didn't you tell us you were coming, and why are you here?"

"Well Mum, you look more stunning today than the last I saw you," Uncle Phillip replied breezily.

"This may be true, but that blarney did not answer my first question," she replied, recognizing his effort to change the subject with his charm.

"I was a bit busy, putting the kibosh on some hooligans that was trying to take over me hometown, my lovely. I wanted to come this year because an old pal of mines' lad is the Grand Marshal this year." Uncle Philip answered her quite sincerely.

"Sounds like a story to me," she declared, raising her eyebrow again. "Why did you ship us this box of Irish mints if you were planning to come here?"

"Have you seen what it takes to get anything through an airport now a day? Besides that they would have charged me double to place it in baggage and that wouldn't have guaranteed it would even arrive. I knew that the Banshee would see that it made it here whether I did or not," Uncle Phil explained.

"I suppose you can stay here for a few days, but NO SHENANIGANS. NO Cailins, Colleens, Abigails, Mollys or Kates running around in our house in their skimpy attire. NO TEACHING THE BOYS FOOLISH TRICKS. Are we clear with these few rules, Philip?" Senona asked sternly.

"Yes, Mum" he replied meekly.

"Maravilloso!" Senona replied in Spanish, as she often did when she knew things may not always be as they seem. "One more thing, eat the candy in front of us first."

Uncle Philip picked up one of the candies, removed the plastic and placed it in his mouth.

"So sweet and minty, I do pick out the best of the best!" he boasted.

Senona gave him a hug and asked everyone to pick up a box of Irish trinkets and take them upstairs. Jeremy and Max picked up Uncle Philip's bags and showed him to his room, asking him about the Hooligans that he had to fight.

As Senona started unpacking some of the Irish boxes, Luis came up behind her and wrapped his huge arms around her and said, "Why are you so hard on the O'Sullivan Clann?"

She didn't say a word right away but instead nuzzled back into her husband's arms. After a few minutes she looked up at him and pleaded, "He won't get in too much, trouble will he?"

They both laughed lightly and kissed, listening to Philip O'Sullivan tell the boys about the 100 or more Hooligans burning and raiding his birth town and how he alone had to stop the madness.

CHAPTER TEN

SOFIA'S STORY

The day before the festivities of St. Patrick's Day, the morning dew glazed the grass with a lingering touch of winter's chill. Camille didn't notice the cold as she met her father outside on their heated dining porch. Gregory had the travertine and soapstone dining retreat built so that they could join Sofia as she communed with nature all year round. Both Gregory and Camille enjoyed sitting in the natural dining space, logs burning in the fireplace for additional warmth. Breakfasts were the best time for both of them when they were home. Sometimes, over mango juice and coffee, they shared stories of the odd creatures Sofia had taught them about.

This was the day that Camille was going to perform for the Grand Marshal of this year's St. Patrick's Day parade, which would have made her mother very proud. Sofia had loved to sit in Gregory's arms and listen to Camille play. Even at a tender age, Camille was gifted in feeling the music and allowing it to flow through her as she played.

"Isn't this just an amazing morning?" Gregory asked his daughter.

"It is almost perfect," she agreed.

They didn't say another word as they watched the warmth of the sun dissolve into mist the dew on the roses and azaleas.

"I know that she will be listening wherever she is tonight, my dear. Starting with the Irish stepping songs and finishing with Beethoven's Moonlight Sonata will bring a smile to everyone's faces and hearts," her father assured her.

"I miss her so much, Father. I still don't understand all the reasons why they took her away, and why I can't at least see her. It is not fair that the elders can change rules for other things but they could not see it in their hearts to understand why she did what she did!" A slow stream of tears rolled down her face.

"My dear Camille, I too miss her so much. I have asked the counsel a hundred times if they would reconsider their decision but to no avail. My only sense of peace is that she did it for our family, just as Atticus is acting for his. I have felt your heavy heart over the past few months. I need you to know that I am always going to be here for you." These were the only words Gregory could find to reassure Camille:

He could not know what she was thinking or how she was feeling without breaking the privacy trust that they promised each other many years ago. He shifted his chair closer to hers and placed his hand on hers. As he gave her hand a gentle squeeze he felt that she was a little cold and distant, but still listening to every word he spoke. Camille in return squeezed his hand even tighter, which brought a welling of moisture to his own eyes. It was at this moment that he knew that if he thought these past few months were difficult, then the next 5 years until she left for college were going to be overwhelming.

"Thank you, Daddy. We will get through this, I know," Camille replied more calmly.

It had been a while since he had heard her call him Daddy. Since Gregory was an elder of the seers and mystics, he was received with such formalities that even Camille had only called him father. He recognized that she was reaching out in trust to him, through her pain.

"We will get through all this in time, but that doesn't mean that it will ever feel any better, maybe just easier to understand." He tried to display fatherly strength and nobility. "I mentioned to some of the others about coming over for a swim early today, if the water is not too cold for them. I can work from here if you want them to visit," he offered.

"I think that might help keep my mind off other things for a while. I will call them after I clean up breakfast," Camille agreed. "Oh, one thing I forgot. Do you think I can bring Lilith tonight to hear me play in the Lucas Theatre? Please?" she begged.

"I am afraid that is one thing that I cannot approve. Even though she would do no harm as far as I know, it is not our venue and some of these people as pretty... let's just say fussy! I am sure that she has heard you play all these pieces a hundred times and loves them all," Gregory decided firmly.

"It was worth a try," Camille shrugged, a wry smile on her face. "I will see if Gretchen's dad can pick up Jeremy and Ethan. I think Ms. Helen is helping Jeremy's mom get things ready for the morning."

Ethan was dropped off by his mom as she made her way to Senona and Luis' house; Gretchen arrived shortly after with Jeremy. Gretchen's father decided to stay and talk with Gregory while Camille, Gretchen, Ethan and Jeremy headed into the living room to listen to Camille practice the pieces that she would be playing that night.

"I can never get enough of this space," Gretchen said to Camille. "It is so awesome, the beautiful statues and huge paintings on the walls and the chandelier!"

"We like it too; you know my father has collected art and antiquities for many, many years. He says it is about the stories within the art as much as the pieces themselves," Camille explained.

"I can tell you the story within that one," Jeremy said smiling. He was looking up at a painting of a partially clothed woman lying on a bed asleep as a distinguished man dresses and heads to the door.

"You boys can only think of one thing, can't you?" Gretchen said shaking her head.

"Hey, don't get me in the middle of this," Ethan protested as Gretchen gave him a little shove.

"That painting is a special one. My father

says it is an interpretation; I don't think the artist was in the room. So who really knows what happened?" Camille replied. Both boys just looked confused as Lilith pounced onto Camille's lap.

"My father says that Lilith can't come to the concert tonight, because a lot of the people there are not as open-minded as we are. They can take their dogs and cats to the mall, grocery store and lunch but I can't take poor Lilith to see me perform in a beautiful theatre for 30 minutes. It's not fair," Camille sighed as she stroked Lilith's fur and placed her on the stool beside her.

Camille picked up a tablet from on top of the piano and scrolled through it briefly. She then placed the iPad on the piano in front of her and touched the screen.

"No need to have a page turner anymore," she said smiling at the others. Camille's fingers danced over the ivory keys of the piano like butterflies over blossoms. They seemed weightless and she played effortlessly. The baby grand piano was old but well maintained, as was apparent by the beautiful music that rang out and engulfed the entire room. They listened, quietly at first, to the Celtic dance pieces and then stood, tapping their feet and snapping their fingers to the music.

After several Irish songs Camille stopped and shifted the bench a bit. Lilith pounced down from the bench and jumped up onto a marble table displaying a lovely china doll, not even touching it as her tail wrapped back around her.

Camille turned off the iPad, moving it from the piano to a brass music stand behind her. She stretched her arms and fingers and took in a large breath of air.

Gretchen, Jeremy and Ethan sat back down in anticipation. Camille told them to imagine that they were outside in a field like the one they collected flowers from on Beltane, but that it was late at night and the sky was clear and full of stars. They could feel the tingling of the midnight hour in her voice.

Ethan heard her silent whisper in his thoughts. "This is for you, Mother."

Her hands hovered for a moment over the white and black ivory keys of the piano.

Lilith purred loudly, as Camille's fingers started to slowly make their way up and down the piano keys. They all closed their eyes, even Camille, and drifted away with the music. Their breaths grew shallow as they felt themselves cross the planet, floating on waves, through dim moonlight where time stood still. After what seemed like forever but was only little more than six minutes, the movement shifted to a faster pace.

The piano stopped suddenly and they opened their eyes. Everyone was in a different spot in the room than where they had started. More concerning was that Camille was resting her head on the ivory keys, sniffling as her chest heaved in and out rapidly. Gretchen immediately sat beside her friend and comforted her as the boys stood guard quietly. Two minutes passed before Camille moved the hair from her face and gained enough composure to speak.

Clearing her throat, she muttered, "Sorry." She paused, and then continued. "That piece was composed by Ludwig Van Beethoven and is called 'Moonlight Sonata'. It was a piece that my mother played often. She had started to teach me it before she was taken away."

The silence was broken from a voice behind them. "It was beautiful. Your mother is so proud of you, my dear. Ms. Hill has done an excellent job of continuing the teaching." Gregory had walked through the parlor with

Gretchen's dad to listen to his daughter play one of his favorite classical pieces.

"We will be reviewing some paper work on the upstairs balcony," he continued briskly.

"Yes, Father. My best friends are here and I am sure that they will help me get rid of my jitters," she responded.

"Very well. Remember that Ms. Hill will be here around five this evening to warm you up," he added.

"Yes sir, I will be ready," Camille replied as the two men climbed the stairs to Gregory's office.

"That was all kind of strange, don't you think?" Jeremy asked aloud.

"Do you mean the floating around to the music?" Gretchen asked.

"Well yeah, that was kind of fun. I really meant the fact that we all kind of liked classical music, and to be honest I can't stand it when my dad plays it at the house. Now if it were pop rock then I could have been dancing on the ceiling," Jeremy replied.

There were a few awkward moments of silence as they looked at him. No one wanted to admit that they enjoyed classical music either, but they couldn't hurt Camille's feelings.

A. DRAGONBLOOD

A smile gradually formed on Camille's face and she started to laugh.

"It's alright. I would prefer to listen to Katy Perry, Black Eye Peas or The Rolling Stones myself. The classical music is just so much more awesome to feel and play than new music. I think if the pieces had words, they wouldn't be as awesome," Camille decided.

The others agreed, then started talking about Eminem's new single, and how Selena Gomez should play a concert near them and how crazy would it be if Britney Spears and Ke$ha did a song together. The arguments about which artist was the best performer continued while they changed into swim suits.

After a few minutes of getting used to the water, they played around with the pool toys while Gregory and Anthony watched from the upstairs balcony. After a while, Camille suggested that they follow her down to her secret place. She gave her father a sign, informing him that she was alright and that they were going to the Hive, as she called it. He nodded wordlessly and the four kids make their way it to the Hive.

"I don't know how many times I have been

here but I still think it is totally cool!" Gretchen exclaimed.

"Me, too," Ethan and Jeremy said in unison.

Camille gave each of them a towel that she had brought down in waterproof bags. "It is pretty amazing; I still don't understand how my father and mother had it designed with the water seal. Apparently, my mother knew something that woodland animals use to seal their burrows near rivers in the spring. My father worked it out and made what he calls a plasma aqua pocket," Camille explained.

"Sure, whatever. It just goes to show you that more people should like us because we can do really cool things," Jeremy said smugly.

Camille took a little plastic pill bottle from her waistband and placed it on a table inside the Hive. She then took a zip lock bag out of her other pocket and carefully removed three camellia leaves, three holly berries and three tea olive blooms. The others watched as she placed them on three small tea saucers that were probably from a set that was hers when she was younger. She then opened the medicine bottle which contained a little sugar, some oatmeal and one used tea bag. She proceeded to place equal amounts of each item on the saucers, and then placed the tea bag on an ocean sponge in the middle. The others watched closely.

She asked the others to close their eyes for a moment, and after a little chant they opened their eyes to see that Camille had changed into a beautiful little sparrow. She shook her body rapidly and three feathers flew off her, floating gently in the air. Each of the others grabbed one. They closed their eyes again as she morphed back into her more recognizable form and put on her swimsuit. Each of them handed her the feathers, which she placed beside each saucer and added, "Come out now, my beauties."

Three small, exquisite fairy-like creatures buzzed around the children's heads for a fleeting moment, before making their way to Camille and perching on her lap and shoulder.

"I promised I would bring you something the next time I was here," she told them.

They flew over to the table to examine their treats. They jumped, spun, danced and make very high pitched sounds that Camille understood clearly. It was obvious that they were excited.

"It is like watching a movie or looking at a picture book every time I see you do that, Camille. How do those writers know that is exactly what they do when they are excited?" Gretchen asked.

"You are assuming that the writers are humans or not like us," Camille replied confidently, knowing that she asked her mom and dad the same things years ago. Gretchen nodded.

"I understand the gift of the sugar for the sweetness, the tea olive bloom for the scent, the oatmeal and tea bag for their skin, and camellia leaves for their bed. But I don't understand the holly berries and the feathers," Jeremy asked curiously.

"You sound like your mom when you ask questions like that, Jeremy," Camille commented. "That's not a bad thing, but it does remind us you are a witch's son."

Jeremy shrugged his shoulders, while the little creatures seemed to be laughing at him.

"First thing they are not gifts, they are treats. A gift would imply that I was bribing them to stay here to light and protect the Hive. So, the holly berry is because it is pretty and they like bright colors and can't carry something that big down here themselves. The feather is strictly for fun, they like to fan each other with them, tickle each other and sword fight," Camille explained. They laughed, picturing the little things zipping around sword fighting and tickling each other.

"Plus, it has your energy in it," Ethan added softly. He had been pretty quiet since hearing Camille play the piano.

"That is why I toss it for them myself, if I can." Camille replied. "I can't always get the right animal but the older I get and the more I practice the better it seems to be."

Ethan smiled awkwardly at Camille. She knew something was bothering him.

"Have you heard from your father about the DM's or anything since the last time you told us?" Camille asked him. DM was the symbol that Camille and Tyson had made up to refer to the Mirror Men. They had started calling them the M and M's, but that made some of the kids think of candy. Since candy was not scary, they had to come up with an alternative abbreviation – the DM's.

"No, I haven't heard from him, but my mom has. She feels that it is better if she communicates with him since she is better at shielding than I am," Ethan replied.

"That makes sense. I just wonder why they are not telling us much and if it is really as serious as they thought," Camille mused. "So what is bothering you then?"

"It's not the right time to talk about it." Ethan answered. He was learning from his mom that there are good times to talk about things and not so good times. In the past he was known for what they affectionately called verbal diarrhea.

"When you got here you were pretty excited," Camille persisted, "but since I played the piano you haven't said a handful of words. That is not easy for you, Ethan."

"Fine then, if you really want to go there!" Ethan burst out. "YOUR MOTHER! I don't know what happened to her. You don't really talk about her; no one does. I hear you talking to her in your head sometimes but I am pretty new to everyone's secrets," Ethan added looking at Jeremy and Gretchen.

The Hive got extremely quiet and even the little fairy creatures disappeared.

"I'm sorry, Camille." Ethan sighed. "Let's just talk about tonight and St. Patrick's Day."

"Yeah, did I tell you that my dad's distant cousin Uncle Philip O'Sullivan is here from Ireland? He got here yesterday; my mom is a little worried about him being here because he is a mischief maker or something like that. He was telling me and Max about these hooligans that he had to fight off from his town before he could leave," Jeremy said, in a hurry to change the subject.

Gretchen didn't know what to say because she heard stories about what had happened to Camille's mother but didn't know what was truth or myth.

"My mom is really worried about Uncle Philip starting shenanigans, as she calls it," Jeremy continued with forced cheerfulness. "Apparently, he has girlfriends named Cailin, Colleen, Abigail, Molly and Kate, who must be pretty hot since she didn't want them coming by the house!"

"Alright Jeremy, enough! I know what you are trying to do and thank you but I should probably tell Ethan, and set the record straight with you and Gretchen about my mother," Camille sighed.

She pulled her hair back into a ponytail, wrapped the damp towel around her a little tighter, and sat down. Jeremy knew that he had said enough, and the other two weren't saying another word.

"Ethan, I am sorry that I made you feel

that way while playing the piano. I have been thinking a lot about my mother lately. It has been harder not having my mother around to help me as my life changes and my body changes. I am a year or two older than you, remember. I wish every day I could talk with her or just place my head in her lap.

"Family is so important is our world and I see others with mothers and fathers, or two mothers or two fathers and some of the younger ones still have grandparents. It makes me sad, angry, and confused. I don't want my father to remarry just so I can have a mother. I want MY mother back in our happy strange little family." Camille stopped for a second to take a deep breath.

She continued. "I was pretty young when it all happened and much of it started before I was even born. My mother was very happy as a young woman. She was born many years ago as a nymph/elf hybrid; she is not immortal but does age at a slower rate than humans. For many years she would play in the forest and along rivers and lakes, unconcerned by being seen because her beauty was that of an angel or a dream. She moved with nature and the seasons.

"One year, as she was travelling the

woodlands and swamps of Georgia, my father (who was still just a boy) saw her. Her petite, breath-taking beauty captivated him in ways he could never understand. They played in the forest for the rest of the summer, until his vacation ended and he had to return to school. Their friendship continued and grew each year he spent at his family's summer home.

"But she had another friend, someone more like her, not human, and not seasonal. My mother enjoyed this *pooka*, but when my father's family returned every year she shunned his attentions, making her preference clear.

"One year my father informed her that they would be leaving early to return to England. His mother was ill and he would have to help care for her before he returned to school. He was only a teenager but he was researching medical books to help diagnose her condition. His selfless love and kindness made her want him for the rest of her life. As he turned to walk away she reached out and gave him a kiss. That kiss, I am told, was a transfer of gifts, giving him senses of the enlightened ones."

Camille shuffled on the stone bench,

unconsciously seeking comfort as she pressed on with her tale. "The *pooka* saw her kiss my father, which angered him because he wanted her for himself. Even though he lived in the forest and played alongside her daily, he knew that the human had captured her heart.

"The next summer my father was not able to return. That year in school, he had been able to sit with medical professors and help them develop a diagnosis and treatment for his mother, through his new insights into the higher realms. He stayed with his mother when he returned from school. The *pooka* would tease my mother by pretending that the human was in the house but did not want to play with her anymore. She was not permitted to venture more than 20 steps away from the tree line or she may not be able to return, so she could not verify his story.

"The next summer, my father and his family were late arriving due to an airline strike. My mother feared that he may not come or even remember her. The *pooka* saw this as an opportunity to make her his and his alone. He told her that he, too, was going to be going away for a while but he would be back in time to move for the winter. She was determined to wait for the boy to arrive for summer.

"My father came to the tree line of the family property as soon as he arrived and called out for her. The new moon had cloaked his arrival. My mother shared her loneliness from his absence and her faith in his return. My father told of his time caring for his mother before she had passed away. His heart was heavy. She pulled him close and tears filled her eyes for my father's loss. Then she led him into the forest where she welcomed him into her hollowed-out tree and he spent the night in her arms. When she woke in the morning, he was gone. She knew that night was the beginning of their new relationship; they were no longer children.

"She hurried to the wood line to find him and saw my father stepping out of the car with both his mother and father. He ran to the forest edge.

"'Sofia,' he whispered into the trees, 'Sofia, I am back like I promised.' Confused, she stepped from the trees, asking why he had told her last night that his mother had passed. He shook his head, assuring her that the gift she had shared with him had helped him save his mum. He reached for her hands, eager for her company, when a harsh noise interrupted them.

"The *pooka* stepped from behind a tree and boldly told him that he did not want him talking or looking at his girl anymore. He announced that they were going to be having a child together. She looked at my father and then the *pooka* and cried out at his cruel trickery. He had used magic to take her. All the creatures of the forest wailed with her, a horrific sound.

"He smugly said, 'Indeed, I used magic and all I had to do was kill some fat local goats for a goblin in exchange for one magic spell. Goblin was surprised that all I wanted was to look like the ugly human that he watched you talking with over the years.'

"The extremely jealous *pooka* told her that it was what she really wanted anyway. He declared that if he ever saw her talking to that, or any, human male again he would cage her for the rest of her life. My father introduced himself as Gregory and reminded the *pooka* that since the trick was malicious, he would have karma to deal with someday. The *pooka* kicked a stick at my father. My father vowed he would be back every year until she was free of his grasp, for their love was pure and unbreakable.

"As years passed, Gregory returned to the summer home a little older and wiser. He listened to the creatures tell stories of the evil *pooka* that had no pronounceable name. They shared Sofia's undying wish to be with Gregory but her fears for the forest creatures if she tried to leave. Most of all, she needed to protect her baby girl, who was as beautiful as Sofia herself, with only her sire's dark hair to mark her.

"The summer years after my father graduated from Oxford, he returned to the Georgia house to find that much of the forest had been burned by a wildfire. He asked the resident raccoon that dined on their garbage if harm had come to Sofia or her daughter. They had moved safely inland to escape the flames, the raccoon confirmed. But she had also heard that the goblin was requesting more goats, since many of the wild goats were lost in the fires.

"Apparently, the *pooka* told the greedy goblin that the next night was a new moon; he would kill him the fattest one he could find if he would leave him alone once and for all. In agreement, they made a deal. The creatures of the forest heard of this agreement and planned an escape for Sofia and her daughter. It meant they would have to leave the forest forever. The forest had become more of a prison that a retreat for Sofia and her daughter and my father would be leaving soon, so her decision was simple. Once the *pooka* was far enough away, the creatures helped Sofia and her daughter to the edge of the woods, and the raccoon informed my father of their location.

"He met her at the tree line where they had played for many years. They gazed at each other through the eyes of children despite the intervening years. She still held his heart, wrapped in bonds of timeless love. Her daughter stared with the hauntingly beautiful eyes of her mother. He said nothing, watching her as walk out of the tree line and into his arms. She breathed in the late night air as if it were the first breath that she had ever taken. The three of them got into the car that he had already packed, including a change of clothes for Sofia and her daughter. By the time the jealous *pooka* returned and realized what had happened, the three of them were in a plane crossing the pond to England.

"The *pooka* ran up and down the tree

line for months, cursing every creature big and small for allowing a human to take what belonged to him. So jealous was he that one night he struck a stone so many times that it sent a spark into my father's family vacation house, burning it to the ground."

"So when were you born?" Gretchen interrupted, leaning forward eagerly to hear every detail.

"My mother and father conceived me in London and over the next few years we all were a happy family. My mother taught us all about how special our gifts were and how each of us was unique in nature. My father continued to perfect his gifts too, as well as work and teach my mother about human life. My father was offered a professorship in the United States. He felt how my mother longed for the trees of her native land.

"So, we moved here when I was six and built this house - with safeguards just in case the *pooka* had not moved on. And he hadn't, either. Not long after we returned, he began to aggravate my mother from the tree line. He spit at her and anyone that was around her, and created great chaos whenever there was an opportunity. She never really showed her frustration, especially around my father who she loved so much.

"The final straw was when he struck down our family cat, Lady (Lilith's mother). My sister heard the cry, and the three of us ran to the edge of the property where she was laying lifeless. We could see the muddy hoof print on her fur. My sister and I were crying, part in anger and part in fear. Our mother tried to comfort us with her natural energy, but in the woods we could hear the *pooka* laughing, threatening the same fate upon everyone she loved.

"My sister was so upset, confused and angry that she did not speak to my mother again. Another year passed and my father built a large fence around the property which probably hurt as much as as much as it helped. Still so in love with my father and not wanting harm to come to anyone else she loved, they say that my mother schemed a plan to be rid of the *pooka* at the hands of others so that the karma would not affect her family.

"One autumn hunting season, she helped to organize a class to promote gun safety for young hunters. They would use live ammunition but shoot only at remote controlled, cut-out deer. She knew that the noise would make the *pooka* curious. To insure his presence at the right place she attached a blouse of hers to one of the pretend deer. His sight was not good in the midday sunlight. He would not see much more than shadows but would smell his chance to steal her back.

"That Saturday afternoon, an overly excited young hunter saw only movement as the *pooka* neared the tree line and moved in for his attack. He waited for one more moment, then unloaded two shots into the pretend deer. The bullets continued through the decoy and into the *pooka* at waist height. The *pooka* released a fierce cry as it used all its energy to return to the safety of woods. The young hunter told everyone that he had shot a real deer, although no body was found.

"My mother congratulated him on his achievements, while he bragged about his deer kill. The *pooka,* who was now paralyzed, called for the goblin, handing him my mother's torn blouse. He demanded justice. The goblin promised the *pooka* justice for this crime, for a price. He whispered his demand and the *pooka* agreed.

"Later, the Goblin addressed the elders of the forest and of the others, explaining what

Sofia had done. My father pleaded for my mother's life. He argued that the *pooka* had lied, cheated, destroyed and killed, driving my mother to an insane act of protection for her family. The elders investigated the events and concluded that although the *pooka* did create chaos and unrest for our family, my mother's attempted murder was a far graver crime than his foolishness.

"My father begged for her life, suggesting banishment and isolation in a parallel world. He asked that she be able to keep her gift of insight but be unable to communicate with this world. This would allow her to listen and keep watch on us while we grew as a family. The elders recognized my father's wisdom as a seer and healer, and since my sister and I had unknown gifts, they agreed to his plea.

"My mother and I played Midnight Serenade one last time that night as my father and sister sat beside us at the piano. She gave us each one more hug, holding on to my father for as long as she could. You could feel a cool breeze flow over us, and then they took her away. Shortly after that, my sister left a note saying she couldn't live here anymore. That is all I remember."

Camille sat quietly for a minute, spent from the emotion of story. Her friends sat stunned and numb. The fairies started whizzing around frantically, breaking the spell.

"Oh! My father is about to get into the pool. He has apparently been trying to contact us for over an hour!" Camille exclaimed.

Jeremy was the best swimmer; he told the others that while they put things away he would go up and explain to Camille's father that they lost track of time. Before he left he looked at Camille and said, "Sorry."

As the others scurried to return things to order, Ethan asked Camille one last question. "I am sorry about what happened to your family, but what happened to the *pooka*? I haven't heard anything about him before."

Camille smiled bitterly. "Remember I told you the Goblin whispered something in the *pooka*'s ear? Well, his price was the *pooka*'s body to feast on instead of a goat. I have heard that the minute the elders took my mother, the Goblin took the *pooka*'s life."

"I guess your mom was sort of vindicated, then," Ethan replied.

"I guess, but somehow it doesn't feel that way," Camille replied sadly.

"I have heard all kinds of different stories

about your mother. I am sure it was hard for you to tell, but I am happy I know the truth now," Gretchen offered. "You know, I have been working on my gifts and if you want, I can bring Lilith to your performance tonight in ghost form. You just need to have a talk with her about not purring too loudly."

"That would be awesome!" Camille agreed, hugging Gretchen so tightly that she gasped for air.

CHAPTER ELEVEN

ST. PATRICK'S DAY IN SAVANNAH IT BEGINS...

The sun was not yet up but spectators and revelers alike were ready for another St. Patrick's Day parade in Savannah, Georgia. Head lights beamed and caution flashers blinked in the historic district along the parade route. Families and parade regulars waited eagerly for the 6 am whistle allowing them to set up their tents, chairs, coolers full of food and most importantly, their Irish green.

A few years ago, the city had to ban families and spectators from setting up in the parks and sidewalks the night before the parade. A few overzealous Irish families may have started pouring the Guinness a little too early. However, the new rules didn't stop most of the families from spending the night in their cars or arriving as early as 4:00am to set up their sites, ready to commemorate the death of the Patron Saint of Ireland. Most of the city's police task force didn't mind the anxious guests, as long as they kept their excitement to a dull roar and shared some of their food and decorations with them during the parade.

Jeremy's family set up at the first sound of the whistle. Of course, with Senona's glowing yearly blog, praising how incredibly organized the city and police were during St. Patrick's Day, they probably could show up at 9am and still have their same spot in Chippewa square. Not to mention that Luis had built or renovated half of city counselors' houses and built two of the new downtown playgrounds.

Jeremy asked once why they just didn't use magic and generate an illusion that they had everything set up so no one would take their spot. Then, he reasoned, they could sleep in a few more hours. Senona told him that performing their civic duty was like magic in its own way, without having to deceive anyone. She did often used magic to raise the EZ up shelters, though. They were Luis-proof

169

and she did not like having the live oak tree leaves falling into the containers of food that lined the tables.

Senona, Luis, Jeremy and Max had been waiting and talking with police and other local families for over three hours. Just before 6am, a big guy that worked for Luis and a woman that everyone call Sweetheart arrived to assist in the set up of the tents, tables and décor. Jeremy and his family, including Uncle Philip O'Sullivan, had attended the event last night where Camille performed amazingly. The only complaint was a loud purring cat that could be heard but not seen. After the performance Uncle Philip got into some argument with a past grand marshal, and then told Senona that the two of them were going out to settle it over some Guinness but he would be there to help with set up early.

Senona made it clear to Luis as they unpacked the food that Philip was clearly not present like he had promised and if he had gotten himself arrested then he was going to stay there until tomorrow. It wasn't as if they really needed his help; they had been setting this up for many years. In less than an hour they had two tents with a banner that read 'Everyone's Irish Today', three tables filled with food, beads, flashing toys and even red Irish beards. Under the tables were four coolers of drinks, boxes of more Irish stuff, bug spray, sunscreen and herbs.

At 7:30am Luis and Senona were ready to change into their St. Patrick's Day finest to attend Mass. As they were preparing to leave, a young officer holding up a somewhat intoxicated man stopped them.

"I found him in a doorway on River Street. He said that he was from Ireland and was visiting his family that were in Chip, chip, awoo Square which I figured was Chippewa. Then explained that his family wasn't really Irish but were Spanish and that they think they are Irish on St. Patrick's Day only," the officer explained. "I remember reading your blog on everyone being Irish in Savannah if only for a day, and then saw the banner on the tents that read 'Everyone's Irish Today.' So, I guess he's yours, ma'am," the officer finished.

Luis could see that Senona was not pleased and if it wasn't for Max yelling out "Uncle Philip!" delightedly, she probably would have let the officer take him to a 24hr. holding trailer. They thanked the officer for everything and invited him back later for all the food and blarney he could handle.

As Luis helped detach Philip from the officer's clutches, Philip grabbed the officer by the hand firmly, tapped his Shillelagh on the ground three times while telling the officer that he was a good man. The officer raised his eyebrows as Philip released his grip, falling into Luis' arms. Luis then asked his friend to keep an eye on Philip as he and Senona were now running a few minutes late.

Senona looked at Luis as if to say, "Really?" She reached into an herb box under the table, pulled something out, chanted a mutter and rubbed Philip's head. He immediately fell asleep on the ground under the table. She smiled a half wicked look at Luis and the boys, and then asked Sweetheart to look after the boys until Helen and the other children arrived.

As she walked away, she handed Max Uncle Philip's Shillelagh, telling him to hold on to it until she got back. Max agreed without question and grabbed the Irish walking stick tightly.

Luis and Senona enjoyed their walk back to the house that morning. As the day continued to get brighter and warmer, the crowds for the parade got louder.

"It's all about the parade," Luis said, smiling at Senona.

Luis was right. Even though the St. Patrick's Day celebrations always carried on for several days in Savannah, the real story was the second largest St. Patrick's Day parade in the country. In only a few hours, over 400,000 tourists along with another 150,000 locals would line the streets of Savannah, 10 people deep. Crowds would fill the historic City Market and the famous River Street along with every hotel room and restaurant in and around the city.

Bagpipes and drums would fill the air of the parade route while live bands braved the tourists on three stages around the historic district. First, there was the Mass at The Cathedral of Saint John the Baptist. Even though Luis and Senona were clearly not Irish or Catholic (although it could be argued that the Irish are part Spanish), they always attended the ceremony.

Jeremy would always stay with Max and the others that arrived to help set up. The upside to staying at the tents was that they got first dibs on the food that guests brought and could stash a few extras of what they liked for later. They would be the first kids to get kisses from the pretty girls who practiced with the different colors of lip sticks. Later, they would run out and kiss military men and woman as they marched in formation on the parade route.

After a few snacks, Jeremy and Max walked onto the street and pretended they were marching in formation themselves. Max used the Shillelagh like a drum major's mace, keeping the beat, while Jeremy flipped over a 5 gallon bucket that was meant for garbage and used it as a drum.

By the next hour, Max was conducting 10 more children, including Ethan and Camille, whose father dropped her off before he went to pick up Senona and Luis for Mass. All of them were snapping their fingers, clapping their hands or Irish stepping on the road in front of the tent.

When the crowds thickened, Helen asked them all to come back off the road, sit down for a spell and have a drink. Sitting on a green and gold blanket, Camille observed that she had never really seen the square like this any other year. Today, it looked just like in her dream.

"Sort of like reading a book for the second

or third time," Gretchen commented as she popped in on the blanket beside Camille.

"I knew you were around here somewhere," Camille said, giving her a good morning hug.

"That sounds about right. I want to thank of you for coming out last night to listen to me perform. It was awesome to have my friends there," Camille said.

"You were amazing!" Ethan told her.

"Yeah really cool, but I liked the way Lilith purred and I had this lady sitting beside my mom who though it was my mom's stomach growling. That was funny!" Jeremy added.

"I don't know how you did it Gretchen, but keeping Lilith ghosted out while you were still visible, that was cool. Obviously you have been practicing and that is going to drive your dads crazy," Camille said while laughing.

Staying shrouded by the huge live oaks, Helen walked towards the blanket where the children were talking. They all hushed up and changed the subject. Walking in the sun would not cause her to burst into flames, like many vampire story tellers have written. Her skin was more sensitive to the sun's rays, but also she just liked the filtered light that the live oaks provided.

"Really, guys? Do you think that my mother wouldn't know what we were talking about if she really cared?" exclaimed Ethan.

Helen smiled at the children as she kneeled down on the blanket with them and said, "I didn't need to use my powers to know that Lilith was there last night. As parents, we learn to pick our battles and as long as Gretchen had her shrouded, then no one could say much to us. I don't see a problem taking a cat to a concert. Now a dog - that is a different story," she laughed.

"It is great to see you all in your Irish attire today and looking well rested, even after a late evening. As parents, we were thinking that some of you are old enough to wander around the square on your own this year as long as you stay together and don't get into trouble. We don't believe that there are any signs of the Mirror Men here today," she added.

They all looked at one another as if she was kidding. When they realized she was serious, became very excited.

"Thank you Madame," Camille replied very politely. "We won't get into any trouble, at least not of our making. And we will keep an eye out just in case the DM's come."

Helen nodded and added, "That is the largest purse that I have ever seen you carry, Camille. If you don't want to tote that around all day, I can secure it under the table for you."

"Huh? No, it is not that bad," Camille assured her. "I have my phone, hand sanitizer, snacks, beads, wallet, iPod etc. in it. You never know when I might need them."

"Alright, I want you all to have a great St. Patrick's Day. My first St. Patrick's Day was with Atticus; this will be my first one without him. Of course, he has been to almost every one of them, long before we were a couple. It will be a great day. Although the parade is starting now, it will still take a while for it to get all the way around to us. You don't have to run off right away," Helen told them as she gave Ethan an affectionate hug and walked back over to the tables where Senona had just returned.

"Cool, Awesome, Beast" - just a few of the words the kids exclaimed about their newly-granted freedom.

"You said that it would be nice if our parents would give us some slack this St. Patrick's Day, Camille," Jeremy commented excitedly. "Did you see it in a vision or something?"

"Hey Ethan, that confirms what that pirate said about your dad being around here for many years," Gretchen said, adding, "If your mom said that he has been to almost every one and the parade has been going on here for over 185 years, he's really old!"

"Wow! He looks good for over 200 years," Camille added, despite already knowing his true age.

They hesitated before leaving, they just sitting and talking and watching the adults, including Uncle Philip who was awake now and receiving kisses from a young woman with green hair and red lipstick.

This was the beginning of the day, and it promised to be long and eventful.

CHAPTER TWELVE

THE FRAY OF THE DAY

Finally, they were on their own, darting between partiers along the crowded sidewalk. The others stopped to laugh at a man dressed like a Leprechaun who was trying to do the two-step, but kept falling on his butt. Camille lagged behind and then slipped behind the statue of Oglethorpe in the center of the square. When one of the most popular bands passed, she moved towards the lion at the back right corner of the monument.

She waited.

Two small men appeared, crawling out from under the landscape stones. Leprechauns, just like the passage said, she thought to herself. They left the stone ajar as they hurried into the festivities. The gap was just wide enough for her to grasp the edge and pull the stone away, revealing an underground passage. Without a moment's hesitation, she disappeared into the ground.

The children made their way around the streets in small groups, observing the events and chaos of the day. Ethan, Jeremy and Gretchen returned to the tents to grab a quick snack and check in with Helen. Falling on the blanket with their food, they traded stories about goofy parade spectators and awesome school bands and dancers.

Jeremy turned to ask Camille about her weirdest experience, and noticed that she was not with them. He stood up and looked around, and then asked Max if she had come back with them. He said that he had not seen her.

Jeremy heard Uncle Philip tossing his Irish candies out to the crowds while cracking jokes at the Scottish bagpipes. "You know the Irish gave you Scots the bagpipes as a joke. You haven't got it yet, have ya mate?" Philip said laughing as the piper tried to ignore him.

"Uncle Philip, Uncle Philip have you seen my friend Camille?" Jeremy asked as he pulled on his boisterous uncle's arm.

"Can't say that I have, lad. Did you get her lost?" Uncle Philip replied.

"I don't know. We were together just over there on the other side of the monument and then, well I don't remember!" Jeremy sounded a little more frantic.

"I will talk with the other parents and see what they know. You three retrace your steps; maybe you shall find the little banshee talking it up somewhere. One more thing, what time might it be now?" Uncle Philip asked Jeremy, handing him a handful of Irish candy.

Thinking that the time had nothing to do with finding Camille, he told him it was 12:25pm.

"Good, I will ask around to see if anyone had seen the young Cailin," Uncle Philip decided, walking off.

Exasperated with his uncle, Jeremy collected Ethan and Gretchen. He explained that his uncle recommended that they retrace their steps to try and find Camille. He opened a candy, gave one to each of the others and shoved the rest in his pocket.

As they approached the monument, they looked under tables, around tents, and even on top of the monument.

"This isn't like Camille," Gretchen fretted.

"Something is wrong; do you think it could be the DM's?"

"Here, over here!" A voice yelled from behind a table and tent.

"That's not Camille. It sounds like Max!" Ethan said.

Max had followed them but had looked down, not up.

"Max you are not supposed to be here," Jeremy complained. "You are going to get me in trouble." Max was sitting under one of the lions by the statue.

"It is just like in Mom's book of secrets, a beast guards the entrance," Max explained.

"Beast! What beast - you mean the lion? I think the lion is just a symbol of strength protecting James Oglethorpe's monument. Why were you reading out of Mom's book of secrets?" Jeremy replied.

Still focused on the ground, Max explained that they only had from 12 till 1:00pm on St. Patrick's Day to enter the chamber or the Leprechauns would get them.

"How do you know that, Max?" Jeremy asked, confused.

"Camille left the book open, and I can read," Max stated defiantly.

Ethan looked at where Max was staring and saw a loose pavement stone. Gingerly, he pushed it aside, revealing a black tunnel stretching downward. Camille's words flickered in his memory, confirming his suspicions.

"Max is right. We have to go, now," Ethan decided, looking at Jeremy and Gretchen.

"Leprechauns, beasts, chambers...I know I am going to be in big trouble for this one!" Jeremy exclaimed as he lowered himself and the others into the hole.

"Ok, now that we are in this hole, does anyone have a flashlight so we can see where we are going?" Jeremy asked.

"I thought that all witches could turn on and off lights?" Gretchen grumbled sarcastically.

"If there were lights in the ground, I could turn them on. Even Max could turn them on," Jeremy retorted, still thinking about how long he was going to be grounded.

"My phone has a camera and flashlight on it," Gretchen suggested.

She turned on the flashlight app, revealing a narrow corridor. It was around 5 feet wide with ceramic tiles on the floor and finished walls. They walked for several minutes, the hall appearing larger as they progressed.

Once they were far enough away from the opening (and presumptively, any Leprechauns), Ethan suggested that they try to figure out where they would be right now if they were on the surface.

"I will be in better shape to figure that out when I know what my little brother knows!" Jeremy said, staring at Max intently. "So what is this about all about anyway? Why would Camille sneak into Mom's magical arts cabinet?"

Max stood still, or mostly still; his head was twitching and his leg was shaking.

"Come on, Jeremy. Don't be angry at him. He may have just helped us find Camille," Gretchen cautioned.

"Well, if she was sneaking around my mom's magical things and took off on us, maybe she doesn't need our help. Maybe she thinks that we wouldn't help her, or maybe she feels she is better than us," Jeremy declared angrily. He cracked the wall as he pounded his fist on it.

"Stop, stop, stop!" Max cried. "I saw her there at my party. She pretended not to have been in there but she knew I left a piece of cake in the room. I told Dad."

"I am sorry Max. I didn't mean to get mad

at you like that. So did Dad tell Mom?" Jeremy asked more calmly.

"Daddy said that he would handle it himself and not to upset Mommy's good chi," Max replied, snuffling a little.

"Ok. So it couldn't have been that bad," Ethan decided. "He never said anything to you guys after that, did he?"

"No," Max and Jeremy replied in unison.

"Now that I think more about it, Camille has been acting a little strange the past month or so," Gretchen added. "She doesn't even care about the DM's trying to kill her, she's been losing focus at soccer – and remember how she was obsessing over this St. Patrick's Day parade route in the Serenity Channel and asking about tunnels?"

"I never said anything to you guys, but last month my mom asked me if Camille was acting strange. I told her I didn't really think so and she thought maybe it was just a young woman issue. She has been blocking me out of her head, which is odd because that is part of my training, to speak without sound," Ethan added thoughtfully.

"She told us the story of her mother and had you bring Lilith to the performance last night," Jeremy said, looking at Gretchen.

"How could we be such good friends and missed all that?"

"We are here now; there is a reason for that. I hope we are not too late," Ethan stated, trying to focus everyone.

"Too late, what do you mean by too late?" Max asked, not understanding Ethan's comment.

"It is going to be alright, Max. My father reminds me all the time that everything happens for a reason. Now we just have to find out the reason." Ethan grabbed Max's hand for reassurance.

"Max, what else did the book say? What was Camille reading about?" Jeremy asked his younger brother.

This was one of those times when Max's autism could be a great benefit. When Max was worried, upset or excited about something, he could remember every detail and play it over and over in his head.

" 'The entrance and the exit are the same but different, look down from the beast in the forest that guards from the negative rear - enter here.

" 'Time is short as are the guardians, so stay clear of the blarney, from a dozen add thirty more once a year only here.

" 'It is what you see but not what it is, heart may keep you, and anger may take you. Be honest to those that need to know and be gone before it ends.' " Max recited the words as if he was reading from the book.

Confused, they looked at each other. How could Camille have been so obsessed with coming here and not confided in them?

"Is that all it said?" Jeremy asked Max.

"That was it. But there was a word at the top of the page that I didn't know," Max added.

"Maybe we can help you and that word could help us," Gretchen suggested.

Max crunched his eyebrows and closed his eyes, the effort of memory apparent. Finally, he said, "I can spell it for you - *ASILE de CHAMBRE de TEMPS.*"

Ethan was the first to comment on the words. "My father speaks French and I think that is what this is. You two speak some Spanish, which is close, so we should be able to figure this out. Chamber is the third word. Temps, I know, means time."

"Asile sounds like Asylum," suggested Gretchen. "Since French is sort of backwards to English that would mean this is the *Time Chamber Asylum.*"

As the words sunk in, they slowly realized that this was the otherworld, a part of the underworld between life and the netherworld.

"Do you think that this is the place that they are holding Camille's mom? If so, that explains why she is here and probably why she didn't want us to know," Gretchen offered.

"My father has been here before. I have heard him speak of it to others. Apparently, Jeremy and Max's mom holds the key to this world, so at least we can get out," Ethan replied.

Max blurted, "Be gone before it ends, be gone before it ends - from the book."

"What ends is the better question? Our lives?" Jeremy groaned.

"Stop being so dramatic, Jeremy. We are here to find our friend and help her. That is our first mission; we can worry about the rest as it comes," Gretchen declared, starting back down the corridor. "Let's go!"

"One of you can use my blinking green shamrock necklace as a light," Ethan offered. "My eyes have adjusted and I can see perfectly in the dark now."

CHAPTER THIRTEEN

ASILE DE CHAMBRE DE TEMPS (TIME CHAMBER ASYLUM)

Camille followed the clues she had been collecting over the past few weeks. She made her way carefully through the various halls and corridors of the underworld. She had originally thought that the Asylum where they were holding her mother was beneath the old county education building, across the street from the square where she had left her friends. Now, she wasn't sure. She had been walking through the corridors for some time and still could not feel her mother's presence.

She had been leaving a trail of fresh rosemary to insure that she could find her way back, if she chose to leave. She also packed a shake light flashlight. She wasn't sure what the custodians of the Asylum used for energy and didn't want to take the chance of the batteries dying. The bag included her mobile phone (which did not work underground), a number of charms, and a folded cloth bag with four pockets, containing catnip, rosemary, mudwort and chili peppers.

Packed under the false bottom of the bag were clean chicken bones, two black candles, an astral candle, a snake skin that she found in the woods at Ethan's house, three sheets of parchment paper, a sharpie marker, a plastic baggy of sea salt, a clipping of Lilith's hair wrapped in a cotton cloth, a Mojo bag full of crystals, a vial of lavender oil, two biscuits and two bottles of water. No wonder Ethan's mom asked if she wanted to store the bag under the table, overloaded as she was.

She dropped rosemary, shook the flashlight and paid attention to the floors, walls, and corridors which she was sure would help her find her mother. She had to be careful not to be caught by the custodian watchers of the Asylum. Senona's secret book said that they had no patience for trespassers; the only problem was that she didn't know who or where they were.

Besides the Leprechauns, which left annually for an hour to watch the parade and steal some trinkets, she hadn't seen anyone since entering the chambers of the Asylum. Her thoughts turned to her friends and father, hoping that they were not too worried about her. She knew her visit was going to be dangerous and thought getting them involved would have been selfish. Still, it would have been nice to have them with her for reassurance.

Ethan was leading the way through the corridors of the Asylum as they searched for Camille. Jeremy, Max and Gretchen followed close behind.

"I still can't believe she didn't ask us to help her do this. The only thing I wouldn't have done was to sneak into my mom's magical stuff. I did that once and got caught. I can still taste frog legs and pickle juice, two things I will never go near," Jeremy decided.

"I am sure that she didn't want us to get hurt or in trouble," Ethan replied. "Besides, this is personal."

"Whatever." Jeremy added, "I'm not sure if we will ever find her in this maze, anyway."

No one responded. Max tightly held his

brother's hand counting under his breath, while Gretchen ghosted in and out of the chambers as they walked.

"Wait, stop! Do you smell that? Rosemary – it smells like rosemary!" Ethan exclaimed.

Jeremy had good tracking skills and kneeled on the ground to further investigate.

"Fresh rosemary, too!" Jeremy confirmed. "It's all along this wall and goes down that corridor." He pointed down an even darker passage that seemed to go deeper into the earth. "It has to be Camille, leaving herself a bread crumb trail, but in this case a rosemary trail. She always carries rosemary leaves with her because they limit her from seeing too much, too fast."

"Alright, I guess we follow the rosemary trail," Ethan said.

Max grabbed Jeremy's hand even tighter.

"It's going to be alright little bro. I am not going to let you go, we're brothers forever," Jeremy reminded him.

Camille finally detected a faint sense of her mother. Picking up her pace, she opened a door, which revealed another door, followed by yet another door. Opening one after the other, she paid little attention to anything else.

She raced through a large chamber that held artwork and pieces of ornate furniture piled on top of each other, all covered in layers of dust.

Only one door led out of the room; she slowed as she approached it, even though she could feel her mother's heartbeat behind it. She felt like there were a thousand eyes staring at her. Even the paintings on the walls seemed to be watching her as she reached for the door handle.

Caution gave way to her need to feel her mother's arms around her. The door opened to a secured room poorly lit by a single candle. The room was dank, 10' by 10' square with one window that opened onto a brick wall. A small woman was sitting in a chair in front of the window, looking at, or through, the wall of brick. Camille's pulse raced.

"Come in, my love," the woman beckoned softly as Camille took small steps towards the chair.

"Mother? Mommy, it is you?" Camille cried as she kneeled beside the chair.

The woman turned and smiled. Her golden hair was knotted and unclean, blue shadows circled her emerald eyes, her silken clothing had been replaced by rough, soiled cotton.

But to Camille, she didn't look much different than she had when they took her away.

"Mommy I have missed you so much. I need you at home with me and Daddy," Camille pleaded.

"Oh my sweet girl, I am always with you and your sister. That was the one gift that your father bartered for before they sentenced me. I can still feel and sense everything you want me to feel," Sofia explained gently.

"I am becoming a woman, Mommy. I need you now more than ever. Let me get you out of here. I have studied some of the witches' spells and I know I can get you home with us," Camille said urgently.

"Like your sister before you, you too are growing up so quickly. You are right, soon you will be a woman and things will change again. Your aging will slow down, as we are near immortal. But you will need to be more careful after what almost happened at Beltane last year," Camille's mother warned.

"Yeah, that was kind of scary. Someone or something is out to kill us, we think. We call them the Mirror Men or the DM's!" Camille explained.

Holding her youngest daughter's hand, she explained that it would be wrong for her to leave the Asylum. "I have to take responsibility for my actions with the *pooka*. More importantly, an escape would distract the elders' attention from this new threat."

"If it weren't for that stupid *pooka*, everything would be alright now," Camille protested.

Sofia answered wistfully, "My dear Camille, I have two wonderful, beautiful, smart daughters that obviously love me. Let us not dwell on the past in a negative way."

"Mommy, I'm sorry I just...it just..." Camille stopped as a voice interrupted from the far corner of the room.

"I know the feeling, Sis," the voice commented dryly.

From the shadows slipped a slender woman sporting trendy gothic clothes, dark eyeliner, big eyes, and a smile that mimicked both Camille's and Sofia's. Several amulets hung from her neck and wrists and both her ears and eyebrows were pierced.

"Mercy? Mercy! Is that really you?" Camille hadn't seen her since they had come for their mother. She had heard rumors and had even channeled her one time, but she hadn't seen her.

"It's really me, Sis. I guess we both had the

same idea – great minds think alike, right? Except I had to pay a witch a large chunk of change to get in here. How did you do it?" Mercy asked her sister.

Hugging each other, Camille's answer was muffled in her sister's long dark hair. "Well, I kind of snuck into Jeremy's mom's secret magic stuff and helped myself to information on the Asylum." She babbled nervously about how she had figured it all out.

"My dear, that was wrong of you, so wrong. Senona will never trust you again," her mother admonished her.

"She didn't catch me and I put everything back and I didn't bring my friends because I didn't want them to get in trouble or get hurt," Camille explained, looking between her mother and her sister hopefully.

Before either of the women could respond, the door flew open once more, but no one entered. The sisters stood protectively in front of their mother, ready for anything.

"Come in, before we are all in trouble," Sofia said sweetly, still smiling at the brick wall.

"You go first, no you go–"

Out of thin air popped Gretchen. "We were

so worried about you! Why did you put us through that?"

"Speak for yourself, Gretchen," Jeremy muttered. "I wasn't worried about her, I was just angry because you didn't ask me to help you with this adventure." Jeremy stalked into the room holding Max's hand. Ethan followed close behind.

Speechless, Camille stared at her friends. She was happy to see them but shocked that she hadn't foreseen this in a vision.

Camille replied helplessly, "Well, I couldn't... I didn't want..."

Mercy cut Camille off. "Hey. I'm Mercy - Camille's half sister from the dirty mean *pooka* side of the family. I remember you, Jeremy, but I don't think I know the rest of you."

Everyone stared at Mercy then back at Camille, then back at Mercy again. Nervous giggles ensued from all.

"What's so funny?" Camille demanded.

"You two are so different, but still the same. Dirty mean *pooka* side of the family ...too funny," Ethan admitted.

"Really, Ethan? Well, we are half-sisters and this is our mother. Besides, I came to see my mother by myself as not to get you hurt or in trouble. Now we are all here, including Max,

who is definitely not supposed to be here at all," Camille said defensively.

"Camille, don't be angry or upset with them. They are here because they are your friends. They care about you." Sofia took her daughter's hand.

"Fine. I am sorry. About everything." Looking at Mercy, she continued, "This is Gretchen, my best friend. This is Max, Jeremy's little brother and the one I have a feeling that caught me on his birthday." Max smiled.

"This is..." Camille started.

Mercy interrupted her sister again. "Ethan; Atticus and Helen's little gift child."

"I don't know about gift child, but yes, you are right," Camille affirmed.

"Pleasure to meet you all today, but I did see all of you last night at the performance," Mercy said.

"You were there too?" Camille replied, surprised.

"I couldn't miss watching my little sister play so beautifully. You have come a long way since I last heard you play piano. You were good then; you are great now. I even got tears in my eyes as you played Mom's favorite piece, 'Moonlight Sonata'."

"I heard it too, my love; it was beautiful!

I could feel your fingers glide over the ivory keys as I floated effortlessly in my dream," Sofia murmured.

Camille asked her uneasily, "Why didn't I see this? If I am to be this amazing light of the seers and shifters, then how come I could not see my friends following me, or my sister arriving on St. Patrick's Day to visit you? I have made a mess of everything."

"My child, you were focused too much on what you wanted, not on what you could offer the greater good. You need to allow yourself to be open to everything, but filter it. Focusing on your wants will not allow the universe to help you fulfill needs," Sofia explained as her energy touched her daughter's heart.

"I am sorry that I didn't tell you and that I was sneaky about everything," Camille apologized to her friends.

"So, anyway, this is our Mommy, Sofia. I risked everything to see her again... I miss her so much, and I don't want to leave her again." Camille had tears in her eyes as she introduced them to her mother.

"It is a pleasure to meet you, Ma'am," Ethan and Gretchen said in unison.

"Good to see you again, Ma'am," Jeremy said and Max nodded his head.

"I knew that my daughter would have good friends as she got older. It is truly a blessing to meet all of you. I know you will fulfill your destinies," Camille's mother replied. She still had not turned from the brick window.

Jeremy looked skeptically at Mercy. "So, where did you go and why were you gone so long? Are you here to stay?"

Mercy replied, "I couldn't stay here after what my father did to our family, so I got as far away as possible. Tokyo was my last stop. I was doing some modeling for Gothic Beauty magazine when I ran into Atticus."

Ethan alerted to his father's name. "What about my father, is he alright?" Ethan demanded.

"He is well and so are the others, but there is something going on that is huge. I mean world-wide. These mirror men, or DM's as I heard my sister call them, are multiplying fast and they are targeting us," Mercy explained.

"You mean to kill us, like they tried to do to Camille?" Gretchen asked.

"No! They can't kill her! She just wanted to see her Mommy," Max cried as he ran to Camille and hugged her.

"Atticus doesn't feel like they want to kill us as much as they want to control our kind,"

Mercy replied. "That is partially why I am back for now. I am going to share everything that I know with the children of the others. Later, I will be a part of the search party to find who or what is behind all this."

Sensing that Ethan was ready to interrogate Mercy at length, Jeremy tugged at his shirt sleeve. "Hey, I don't know how long we have been gone but I know that we probably need to get back before I am in even in more trouble," he insisted.

"Jeremy is right. I have truly enjoyed seeing my daughters and meeting their very special friends. You must go now or you will never leave here," Sofia said, still smiling benignly despite her chilling words.

"It won't be that bad, Ma'am," Jeremy assured her. "There wasn't anyone or anything around on our way here."

"They don't mind you coming in, son; it is the leaving that they don't much care for," Sofia commented wryly.

Jeremy swallowed deeply. Max grabbed his hand again while Camille and Mercy hugged and kissed their mother goodbye.

"I have heard talk of those mirror men creatures of which you speak. They need an energy source to survive," Sofia informed her daughters.

"How do you know that, Mother?" Mercy asked.

"They entered the first corridor of the Asylum last year, but by the time that they made it to the first chamber room they were laboring hard. That's all I know before the ghouls took them." Sofia sighed and let go of the girls' hands.

Ethan handed Camille her saddle bag, groaning at its weight. "What do you have in there?"

"I almost forgot! I brought you something special, Mommy." She handed her mother the wrapped hair of Lilith's and a rose quartz crystal, pressing them into her hand before running for the door.

As the door closed behind them, they heard a sweet sound like that of a Moonlight Sonata. The room glowed with a rainbow of colors as Sofia held the crystal in one hand and rubbed the cat fur on her cheek.

CHAPTER FOURTEEN

ESCAPE FROM THE TIME CHAMBER

"Follow the rosemary," Camille ordered as she closed each door behind her, leaving each room as it was when she arrived.

"That's how we found you in the first place," Jeremy barked back, dragging Max and following Ethan, who was in the lead. "Maybe we can get out of here before they notice us. It is St. Patrick's Day; they are probably distracted by the parade."

"Yeah, that sounds right, Jeremy. The custodians and guards of the underworld's Time Chamber Asylum get St. Patrick's Day off every year. Why would any of the permanent residents want to escape to the surface when they have this amazingly grey, dank place to live in for all eternity?" Mercy snapped sarcastically.

"Is he always this dense?" she asked Camille.

"Well, yes and no. He just doesn't think before he says things sometimes. You get use to it," Camille answered truthfully.

Jeremy responded, "I guess when you say it like that it does sound odd. But I know lots of people that get holidays off."

"Right, but none of them are guarding Grendal, Iago, the Wish Wash Wizards, and Lolita, now are they?" Mercy reminded him, shaking her head.

"There is NO doubt that you two are sisters!" Jeremy declared as they both gave him that crunched-eyebrow stare that he had seen so many times before.

They stopped suddenly. A literal crossroads had appeared in the main corridor of the Asylum that hadn't been there before.

"Ok, this wasn't here before," Ethan confirmed.

"Just follow the rosemary," Camille insisted.

Ethan closed his eyes and used his other senses, hoping to pick up the rosemary scent. Nothing. He opened his eyes and looked down each of the four passages. They all looked the same.

"Alright, Jeremy you might not be able to see as well as Ethan, but you are a good tracker. Which way?" Gretchen asked.

"Are you telling me what to do?" Jeremy snapped. "You think that you are better than me because you can disappear? Just because you walk or float through walls and drifting in and out of others doesn't mean anything." He was becoming very upset with her for no apparent reason.

"It's not like that at all, Jeremy," Gretchen replied, disturbed by his response.

"Well, I am better than you because I have more talents than you. If I wanted to right now, I could punch through the ceiling of this room and be back up there watching the parade like I had planned today," Jeremy snorted.

"Obviously something is getting in your head, Jeremy," Camille said. "Sometimes you say things before thinking, but you would never say that to Gretchen, ever."

Jeremy handed Max over to Gretchen and began to jump up and down, pounding the 10 foot high ceiling with his fist on every launch. As he smashed the ceiling, pieces fell to the floor and soon the floor cracked, too. It was hard to say which was going to collapse first.

"He's GARGING out!" Ethan exclaimed.

"It is hard to tell if he is flying or jumping," Mercy observed. "He is part witch and part gargoyle, isn't he?"

"Yes, but this isn't helping us. As a matter of fact, it is probably attracting more attention to us than we would like," Camille replied.

Reaching into her large saddlebag purse, she rustled around until she found a runes pouch that contained a vial. Just before his next fly/jump, Camille rubbed the lavender oil on him and gave some to the others, as well. Jeremy stopped his antics instantly, still breathing heavily.

Jeremy looked at Camille and said, "Lavender, thanks."

"Lavender?" Ethan asked.

"Lavender protects against evil spirits," Jeremy explained. "Sorry about what I said, Gretchen," he continued, head down and looking up through his hair at Gretchen.

"I knew that something must have possessed you. I just don't know what," Gretchen replied.

"Shadow Fleas," Mercy stated. "I have

seen them before. They are nearly invisible creatures that enter unprotected individuals through their nose, eyes or any small opening. They shake off their dust-like skin into your system, creating chaos in your brain. They are considered evil. A wizard created them and used a cat to spread them to his wife, whom he thought was unfaithful."

"That would explain why we couldn't see them," Gretchen said.

"So, if we are covered in lavender now, then we should be able to get out of here without anything evil attacking us, right?" Ethan reasoned.

"Well sort of," Camille clarified. "We are protected from evil doers sneaking up on us like the Shadow Fleas, but we are still visible to the ones that don't care about being sneaky."

"Standing here talking about who will and who won't attack us is not helping us find the path back to the entrance," Mercy observed.

"This way, this is the right way," a small voice whispered. Looking down, she saw Max tugging at her leg and pointing to the right.

"You sure it's that way?" she asked him.

He didn't say anything; he looked up at her, nodding his head continuously.

"If Max says it's this way, then it is more than likely this way. He has the ability to remember details to a fault sometimes, but he's 99.9% of the time correct," Jeremy informed Mercy.

The others laughed because they knew Max's powerful memory all too well. Jeremy didn't laugh as hard because he had firsthand experience with Max remembering things that he would have preferred forgotten.

"We came 164 steps, turned right, went 1220 steps and one jump then turned left, then 54 steps straight, turned left again for 2580 steps, opened a door and went through, another door, door, door, stopped," Max told Mercy.

"So we have gone 2580 steps and now we have to go right 54 steps?" Mercy asked Max.

Max nodded his head and with a smile reached for her hand. Mercy was quite a bit taller than Max and the others. Her height obviously came from the *pooka* side of her family since Camille and their mother were not nearly as tall. Mercy shrugged, reached down and grabbed Max's hand and led them down the way he pointed.

They continued 54 steps and just like Max had said, there was a corridor where both

Jeremy and Ethan picked up the rosemary scent again. In less than 1500 steps from the entrance to the Time Chamber Asylum, they stopped.

"Did you hear that?" Gretchen asked nervously.

"If you are talking about the somewhat deafening wailing sound, then yeah, we heard it," Jeremy replied.

The ear piercing sound seemed to be coming from in front of them and getting closer. It quickly became so loud that they could not hear each other. Camille used Ethan's gift of whisper speech to ask what he saw down the corridor.

Ethan concentrated. When the creature finally came into view, he began waving his arms frantically. In whisper speech, he told them 'back, back.'

Hearing the terror in his voice, they turned around and followed him at a run back down the corridor. They passed the right turn that they had taken to get that far. As they ran the sound faded, and although their ears continued to ring they could hear each other again. They stopped when the corridor ended, leaving them a choice of turning left or right.

"What did you see back there?" Gretchen asked Ethan.

"More than one, maybe four women-like creatures with shiny wings and scaly skin. I think they had horns, but they definitely had fangs. I could see the long snake-like fangs in their mouths as they screamed," Ethan panted.

"Banshees," Camille said, shaking her head.

"Gorgon," Jeremy corrected her.

"Gorgon wouldn't scream like that, but I haven't heard of Banshees having scaly skin and fangs before," Mercy informed them.

"See, it had to be Gorgon then," Jeremy concluded.

Ignoring him, Mercy continued. "Everyone knows that since Medusa had her head cut off there are only two Gorgon left. Ethan said that he saw at least four of them. So if the Gorgon have mated with Banshee offspring, this is a new creature, or at least not a 3000 year old one, anyway."

"Whatever it is, they didn't want us to go that way. So where are we going now?" Gretchen asked. "It makes sense to go right again if we are trying to get back to the entrance," she suggested.

"Let's see where it takes us, but I have a feeling that we should be going left instead," Jeremy said.

After only a few steps down the corridor, they thought they could hear the celebrations of St. Patrick's Day just ahead of them. Just the thought of returning to the festivities of the day made them hurry their pace, eager to leave the dank, dreary Asylum. Strangely, the farther they ran the more their excitement was replaced by anxiety, even terror.

Camille looked hard at Mercy, declaring, "I am never going to be as beautiful as you."

Mercy responded, "You are the one that everyone loves the most. You succeed at everything you do - school, soccer, music, shifting, seeing. Is there anything that you can't do?"

Ethan froze and began yelling, "Get them off me!" Gretchen was flashing in and out like a strobe light at a dance.

Jeremy stopped and turned to Max. "You never get in any trouble for anything that you do. Why can't you just do something wrong once in your life? Everyone worries about how your autism is going to affect your gifts; well, I think it gives you an edge over me."

Max just stared at Jeremy, confused.

Whatever was creating this unrest was not affecting him. He had never had to help or save anyone before but he thought that there must be something that he could try.

Max remembered what he read in his mother's book about 'the corridors of the Asylum removing the joys of your life, while making one compare theirs to another that they wish to emulate.' His big brother was definitely not joyful, and he sounded like he was comparing himself, so maybe that was what the book meant.

The book said that you had to carry rosemary in your hand to help break the spell, but the rosemary was way back where the other creature had been wailing away. Rocking back and forth Max thought hard as Jeremy continued to compare himself to Max and the others. Where was he going to get rosemary? Was there something else he could use?

Camille and Mercy were getting louder in their criticisms. He saw that Camille had put her bag on the ground, and wondered if there could still be rosemary in it. Unnoticed, Max grabbed the bag and reached deep into it. He pulled out a folded bag of herbs. Sniffing the herb in the first pocket, he shook his head, knowing that it wasn't rosemary. Rosemary smelled like the Italian restaurant that his family enjoyed eating at on occasion.

The second pocket was rosemary.

Now he had to get the rosemary into everyone's hands long enough for them to snap out of this trance. He started with Jeremy, who was still recalling all the things that Max did well. He gave him a hug and placed the rosemary in his brother's pocket. Jeremy stopped talking, shook his head and gave Max a big hug.

"Hey, what happened?" he asked.

Max pointed to the bag of rosemary and then to the others, still entranced. Understanding immediately, Jeremy helped Max distribute it to the others. Exhausted, they leaned against the wall and sighed in unison.

"Wish we had something to eat," Ethan said.

"I'm hungry too," Gretchen agreed.

Camille dug around in her saddle bag and pulled out the two biscuits and the water that she had packed earlier.

They all gave her a peculiar look but only Jeremy was brave enough to say, "Is there anything that you don't have in that bag?"

Returning their looks, Camille explained that she wanted to be prepared for anything.

They decided to split the biscuits up between them and only drink one bottle of water, just in case they were there longer than they expected.

"Hey, I have a pocket full of Uncle Philip's mints. He gave me, like, a million before we came down here. If anyone needs fresh breath or a sugar fix, I'm the go to guy," Jeremy offered, trying to lighten the mood.

"What about Uncle Philip?" Camille asked. "Did you tell him and our parents that I was down here or something?"

"No! Well, not exactly. I mean, I told him that you were sort of missing but he doesn't know where we are," Jeremy explained, looking at Ethan, Gretchen and Max but not her.

Camille knew Jeremy's poker face. As soon as he took his eyes off her and looked at the others for reassurance, she knew that he wasn't telling her everything.

"It doesn't really matter anyway. I saw my mother and Mercy is back and we are almost out of here, I think. Then I am going to have to deal with your mom and my father. I will take responsibility for all of you coming and looking for me," Camille decided.

"We are all in this together," Gretchen replied.

"We chose to come looking for you. You didn't make us do anything," Ethan added.

Jeremy placed his hand on Camille's shoulder and said, "We joke around all the time, poke at each other but that is what family does with one another. We are all a weird and wonderful family in my eyes."

"Mine too," Gretchen added.

Max nodded vigorously and Ethan added, "I don't have a sister or a brother but Jeremy is right. I consider all of you, even Mercy, my family."

Mercy placed her hand between Camille's downcast eyes and the floor, capturing each tear as it fell.

"We are leaving our energy behind for them to use against us," Mercy warned as she wiped her sister's tears on her jacket sleeve. "I am sorry that I left you and Gregory when I did, but I had my reasons. I thought about you every day, Sis. It is great to see that you have a great family of friends here."

"What was that?" Ethan heard something on the other side of the wall.

"It is probably time to start moving again anyway, if we have any chance of getting out of here today," Jeremy said.

"We have to get out today," Camille stated.

She knew something that the others didn't. "The legends say that if a visitor doesn't leave the Time Chamber Asylum the same day that they entered, they will be cursed to spend all eternity in the underworld looking for a way out."

"In that case, let's get a move on!" Jeremy urged.

"It is apparent that we are not going to get out of here the same way we got in," Ethan observed. "I suggest that we head in this direction and keep our eyes, ears and every other sense we have open for anything that appears to be a way out."

In agreement, they continued on. Gretchen spent much of her time popping in and out of rooms and above and below the corridors, looking for alternative routes. But every room looked identical to the last and each hallway was a copy of the one they were travelling.

Camille gave Max a piece of the parchment paper and a sharpie. She asked him to draw their route, so they would know where they had been already.

They began to pass others wandering the corridors. A set of twin brothers that were attached at the hip. A fairy that followed them for a while until Camille gave her a gem stone from the bag. A dog that walked on its hind legs and insisted that he knew the way out but was choosing to stay for a while.

Camille stopped in front of a particularly large puddle of murky water on the floor. "I have an idea."

She pulled out the bag with the four pockets of herbs from her purse. "I forgot my mirror, but this should work just fine," she said, sprinkling the mudwort around the puddle.

They all knew that mudwort was used by seers and mystics to improve their visions. It was dangerous, though, and could be as addictive as a drug if used too much. Very few children were permitted to use it.

"Are you sure about this?" Jeremy asked Camille hesitantly. Someday he would have to learn to use the magic of the herb to foresee the future but until then he was perfectly happy letting others do it for him.

"I know that it can be a dangerous gift of nature, but in my realm this is like chewing gum and walking at the same time," she assured him.

Ethan lit the black candle as instructed by Camille. He held it close to the puddle, careful not to block it. Camille stared at it, going deeper and deeper into a slumber state. Mercy and Gretchen held her steady. After a few minutes, she gasped and bounced up to her feet.

"You saw our way out of here!" Jeremy guessed excitedly.

"Not exactly, but I do know what we are looking for," she explained.

While packing things back into her bag, she removed something else and placed it in her pocket. She told them that they were not far off. They were looking for a large, heavy brown door with oversized metal hardware.

"Come on, this way." Camille led them down yet another corridor into a small room. The next door was only 50 paces away.

Halfway across the room, Ethan noticed eyes on the walls, watching them. His vision sharpened and detected bodies attached to the eyes - big bodies.

"There are huge creatures in the room with us right now," Ethan whispered. "By chance did you see this in your vision?"

"Yeah, I kind of did," she admitted. "They won't harm Gretchen, Mercy, Max or me, though. They would prefer to keep us as wives someday and Max as a trophy. They would, however, like to eat you and Jeremy," Camille added.

"How many do you count?" Jeremy asked Ethan.

"Too many for you and me to handle alone," Ethan replied tersely.

"Bring it on," Jeremy said as he started to Garg out a bit.

"I was afraid you were going to say that," Ethan responded.

"I was hoping he was going to," Camille stated. She pulled out the sack of herbs once again.

As the creatures moved closer, their shapes became more prominent. They were hell hounds, big hell hounds. Ethan's eyes started to glow a yellowish red, his shoulders seem to spread, and yellowish fangs pressed down from him upper gum line. His fingers cracked as he stretched every muscle in his body.

Jeremy was already double his normal size. He also had fangs, both upper and lower ones. His arms looked like cannons and sounded like thunder as he crushed them together.

"What do you think?" Jeremy said, his voice deeper yet still youthful.

"I still think there are too many of them for the two of us," Ethan replied. "You are looking pretty buff, though."

"You can't kill them. Just get us all through the door. Don't kill them; it is not allowed, if we want to get out." Camille shouted. "Hey, Jeremy, Ethan - open up."

They turned to look at her, their mouths open already. Camille filled their mouths with a dry leafy herb.

"What is this stuff?" Ethan asked, chomping away.

"Catnip!" Camille replied.

Distracted by her answer, he missed the first hell hound's lunge. He was knocked back effortlessly. Jeremy pushed one, then two, then three hell hounds back. Ethan returned and dispatched two more as they kept moving towards the exit door.

"Catnip is an ancient herb that warriors would chew or drink as a tea before a battle," Jeremy explained to Ethan as he clobbered another hell hound that jumped him from behind. "Can't you feel the additional power and keen senses that you have right now?"

Ethan looked around. Jeremy was right, every sense was more acute. He could feel the blood rushing through his body; every sound rang more clearly. The stench of the corridor was worse and the sound of the hell hounds' whine after they stopped them was more intense.

Turning more quickly than he ever had before, Ethan slashed a hell hound and sent it tumbling to the far wall.

"Come on guys, enough. We are through. They won't follow us past this room," Camille called.

"One more - there is one more coming at us right now. I am going to take care of this persistent mutt," Jeremy declared.

"Just slow them down Jeremy; we have to go," Ethan reminded his friend, as they were now back to back fighting the hell hounds.

"I feel so good, so alive. The older I get the stronger I have become, but this is awesome. I could pound these hounds all night long," Jeremy cried.

"Don't kill them Jeremy. You can't kill anything in the Asylum and they can't kill us. The Asylum lives off the energy of everything in it. If you kill anything the balance will be thrown off and I don't know what will happen to us then," Camille explained from the doorway.

"They are trying to kill us, I am sure of it," Jeremy argued.

"No, they are just trying to stall us from leaving," she retorted worriedly.

Jeremy shrugged his huge shoulders and lifted his foot to the mouth of the last hell hound, launching it clear across the room. Ethan turned and looked for it, if only to see that it was still breathing. It was taking short, shallow breaths.

"Now, let's get out of here with the others!" Ethan exclaimed.

Once through the doorway, Jeremy continued to flex and hop, like a trained prize fighter. Mercy extended her hand to him, as if to shake for a job well done. As soon as Jeremy grabbed her hand, she reached for Ethan's. She scraped her foot along the floor like a bull preparing to charge, then stopped quickly and stomped once. A charge of energy raced through their bodies like lightning, making them hurl the remnants of the catnip onto the floor. They rapidly returned to their regular size and senses.

Jeremy reached in his pocket for one of Uncle Philip's mints that he had been enjoying all day and handed one to Ethan, telling him that it would help with the dry mouth.

"That was crazy awesome! Well, except the part where I hurled," Jeremy said, sucking on the mint. "What about you Ethan - pretty beast, right?"

"Yeah, pretty beast. I will have to remember that trick in the future. As a matter of fact, if we get out of here I have a lot of new things I can try," Ethan decided.

"We are getting out of here!" Max cried.

"Yes, we are almost there. Just down this last corridor there will be a sign that reads 'Jingle Bells' on a door. We go through that door and there will be another exit just beyond it," Camille explained.

"Jingle Bells? Are you kidding me?" Gretchen exclaimed, popping back in. "It is March 17th St. Patrick's Day - not December 25th Christmas."

"Look I am just telling you what I saw and so far it is correct. I know it seems weird," Camille replied.

They stayed close as they walked down the hall. If anything was left to slow their exit, at least they would be together. The corridor became even darker and a heavy fog lingered in air, making it harder to see. Ethan strained to lead them, thinking how that catnip would sure be nice. His hand started to shake in Mercy's as they continued down the dim lane.

"What is it, Ethan?" Mercy asked, seeing very little but feeling spider webs crossing her face and drips of water trickle down her neck.

"It's the spiders," Jeremy explained. "Ethan is not really into spiders. As a matter of fact, a month or so ago Camille and Gretchen played a trick on him with a very big spider."

"I am sorry again!" Camille said quietly.

Mercy squeezed Ethan's hand and informed him that his father could stop talking about how amazing his son was. She told him that there were already stories being spread about these amazingly gifted children that fought off an invasion of the Mirror Men creations. This group of vampires, witches, mystics and shifters were gathering the young and preparing them for what could be an apocalypse for their kind.

"I came here, but not because of those stories; I know they will come to be. I came back to see my mother, but more so to see the boy vampire, not even of age yet that rose up to fight or sacrifice himself to protect my sister. I have not been disappointed in you. It is an honor to have you lead us through this wretched place with your incredible eye sight, despite the spiders."

Ethan recognized Mercy's effort to bolster his courage, but still didn't release her hand. He walked faster, picking the spider webs from his face and hair. He thought about what Mercy had just told him. He wondered what stories were being told about him, Camille, Jeremy and Gretchen. They were going to play a part in the future of this world, but at the moment he couldn't imagine how.

"I think this mist or fog or whatever is turning into something, or more than one something. It just grabbed my leg," Gretchen exclaimed, tugging at Camille's hand.

"Here, hold on to Max's hand and keep walking," she told Gretchen as she let go.

"Go ahead with Jeremy," Gretchen told Max. "I am going to stay here and help Camille."

"Thanks, Gretchen. We are going to have to do two things at once and move quickly," Camille explained.

"We did it before in Wee World, we can do it again here," she said confidently. They could feel and hear the commotion from the restless energy surrounding them.

"The fog is just the energy from spirits that mean us no harm. They are just a distraction from the other creatures that will hurt us to slow us down. But I have a surprise for them," Camille explained.

"I am going to give you this salt. I need you to take one step in your ghost form and create a sacred circle. On my mark - oh yeah, one more thing, keep your eyes closed."

"On your mark, salt circle, eyes closed - got it," Gretchen repeated.

Camille waited until she knew her friends were far enough away. All she could hear were chattering teeth, low growls and the hiss of the swirling moist fog. She knelt on the damp floor, rolled the snake skin into a circle and placed a candle in the middle of it. Holding two matches in one hand and clutching something else in the other, she gave the signal.

"NOW!" Camille ordered.

Gretchen stepped out and thickly wrapped them in a circle of salt, then closed her eyes and quickly returned to Camille's side.

Shrieks echoed but the moist fog dissipated as Camille struck a match off her zipper. It flickered but went out quickly. She struck the second match, which flared brightly as she pressed it against the wick of the candle. The candle cast a glow which made the creatures appear as disjointed shadows capering around their circle. Neither girl could fully visualize their disfigured boney bodies or billiard ball, washed out eyes, or their yellowed fangs and hairless heads.

Camille counted - one, two, three, four, five. On five, Camille stood and opened her hand, which contained the chili pepper powder from her bag. She spun in a circle using Gretchen as a pivot point, blowing the chili pepper power outward as she rotated. The creatures screamed in pain as the powder burned their eyes and skin. The creatures tore at their eyes and skin frantically as they scurried away. An eerie silence fell abruptly in the corridor of the Asylum.

"It's alright to open your eyes now," Camille instructed Gretchen, who hadn't moved a muscle since she returned.

"What the heck were those things, and what did you do to make them leave like that?" Gretchen asked. She opened her eyes and peered cautiously down the hall.

Camille smiled and told her that creatures

were mutated beasts that she had read about in one of her father's library books.

"How did you know what they were, if you couldn't see them?" Gretchen asked.

"That's the thing, we spend so much time wanting to *see* things. Past scribes and bards recorded information from *all* of their senses. I remembered reading about the sounds these creatures made and how they tricked the spirits into protecting them," Camille explained.

"Wow! I guess I better start reading more and paying attention to the details," Gretchen decided.

"You guys wouldn't be down here if I had paid more attention to things, too," Camille admitted.

Gretchen reached out and took Camille's hand. "Come on, we need to catch up with the others and I have a little trick to do just that."

Camille held on the Gretchen as she guided them both through the corridor like they were floating on a wave.

"This is incredible!" Camille exclaimed.

"We all have our gifts," Gretchen replied with a grin.

Five hundred feet down the corridor they caught up with Mercy and the boys.

"Camille, Gretchen!" Max exclaimed running up and hugging them as they became visible.

"We heard screams echoing through the Asylum," Mercy added, "and we thought, well we thought that you might have...."

Camille interrupted her. "No, I am not going to lose my friends or my sister again."

"How did you get away?" Ethan asked.

"A little old-fashioned pepper spray did the trick. I will tell you what they were at another time; now we have to get through this door and back to the St. Patrick's Day festivities," Camille said briskly.

"Unless you have a universal magical skeleton key in that bag of yours, we are at a dead end," Jeremy said, realizing too late that his choice of words was probably not the most appropriate.

"The key is on top of the frame," Camille replied.

Jeremy hoisted Max, who was the smallest and lightest, up to the top of the huge door frame. Max felt around but could not find it.

"It is not here," Max told them.

Camille rummaged around in her bag,

pulled out the chicken bones and handed them to Mercy.

"Here, Mercy. I know that you have done this a few times before," Camille added.

Mercy was good at picking locks. She was grounded more than once for picking the lock on the library door when they were younger.

Mercy took the bones and expertly manipulated them in the keyhole. Within seconds, the tumblers fell and the lock was open but the door still was jammed.

"Stand back everyone," Mercy ordered.

Everyone moved away as she turned her back to the door. With one swift kick the door flew open. She straightened herself up and caught their shocked stares.

"Remind me not to get behind you when you are mad," Jeremy laughed.

"Nice kick," exclaimed Camille.

"There are some traits from the *pooka* side of the family that come in handy," Mercy shrugged.

"Look!" Max yelled, pointing.

Through the door lay an abyss of human carnage, abandoned buildings and burned fields and trees. They were out of the Time

Chamber Asylum, but definitely not back in Savannah.

"Is this the...Underworld?" Gretchen whispered.

"It must be. We're doomed for all eternity here," Jeremy wailed.

"Enough with the drama, Jeremy," Mercy said, whacking him on the side of the head.

"I don't know about drama, but I do know that those are ghouls and they are coming our way," Ethan observed. "Do you have anything left in your bag to fight against GHOULS?" he asked Camille nervously.

While Camille was rummaging around in her bag, Mercy yelled, "Come on this way, I hear bagpipes!"

Their options were limited – fight off ghouls, return to the Asylum, enter the Abyss or run in the direction of bagpipes. They had to run.

"Those ghouls are pretty fast runners," Ethan exclaimed, panting.

"Imagine chasing down your first fresh dinner in centuries - you would run fast, too," Mercy replied.

"I've got nothing left in my bag," Camille cried. "I'm sorry!"

"Oh no!" Gretchen groaned. "There is

another creature in front of us, blocking the way. It is huge and has a big stick."

Jeremy looked behind them but the ghouls were already close enough to smell. Death and decay lay on either side of their path. Whatever the creature was, it wasn't moving to attack.

"No choice guys," Jeremy confirmed. "Keep running!"

The music got louder as they got closer.

Max suddenly rushed ahead of them all and exclaimed, "That's not any stick. That is Uncle Philip's Shillelagh!"

"Then that must be Uncle Philip," Jeremy exclaimed in relief.

They were still 300 paces from where he stood above them, outlined by drifting fog. The ghouls were only 100 paces behind them and gaining ground, eager to sate their ravenous hunger.

"We may not make it in time," Gretchen yelled.

"Wait! I think he is saying something. Ethan, use your whisper speech thing to hear what he is saying," Camille urged.

"He is telling Jeremy to use the mints. The mints?" Ethan repeated, confused.

"The MINTS? He must mean the mints that he gave me this morning," Jeremy said.

He had been eating them throughout the Asylum to settle his nerves. Now he hoped that he had enough left. Reaching into his pocket, he found 5 mints and 3 mint wrappers.

"What does he want me to do with them?" Jeremy asked Ethan.

"Give them to, I mean throw them at the ghouls," Ethan explained.

Jeremy tossed them over his shoulder in the direction of the ghouls. The ghouls scattered, chasing after the flying mints and forgetting the children as they fought each other for the mints and wrappers.

They clambered up the rocky cliff, avoiding the decayed bodies and crumbling buildings. Several minutes passed before they reached Uncle Philip.

When they finally reached the summit, Camille asked, "What do we do now?"

"This is the really impressive part!" Uncle Philip exclaimed. He raised his mighty Shillelagh over his head, bringing it down and piercing the ground while chanting Erin Go Bragh. The earth rumbled and began to move below them, raising them like an anthill. The sky became a shifting dark curtain, which suddenly parted to reveal an opening to the surface world.

The bagpipes became significantly louder and they could see daylight. As they surfaced in a square away from the parade the first thing they saw was a sign that read 'Jingle Bells Church' and a single bagpiper playing every Irish and Scottish tune he knew.

"Thanks mate," Uncle Philip told the piper and flipped him a solid gold coin.

The piper bit down on the coin to check that it was real, obviously knowing Uncle Philip O'Sullivan all too well.

"Anytime, chap," the piper replied, disappearing into a crowd.

"Jingle Bells, you were right Camille," Gretchen exclaimed. "I remember the story now. James Lord Pierpont wrote the song 'One horse open sleigh' right here in Savannah; we call it 'Jingle Bells'. That mean we are in Troup Square, which also means we are over eight blocks away. We are so in trouble!"

"Not as much trouble as you would be if we weren't here," a voice from behind them said.

The children turned and were greeted by Gregory, Luis, Anthony, and, of course, Uncle Philip.

CHAPTER FIFTEEN

HONOR A PATRON SAINT
&
UNCLE PHILIP O'SULLIVAN?

"So how be this fine day for you younglings?" Uncle Philip asked, shaking the dirt from his clothes. Camille and Mercy looked at their father, Gretchen looked at hers, Jeremy and Max looked at Luis and Ethan just stared at the ground.

"It be alright for you lad to look at me, if you are feeling a bit out of the loop and all," Uncle Philip suggested merrily.

"It's not that, sir," Ethan replied awkwardly. He looked up warily. "I am just still trying to figure out how you did that."

"Did what?" Uncle Philip replied innocently.

"Enough of your goading, Philip," Camille's father chided.

"Philip - Uncle Philip as you know him - is an eternal spirit; he is one of few that can walk in both worlds," Gregory explained. "I asked him to join us this St. Patrick's Day because I knew that only he would be able to save my daughters."

Turning to Camille, Gregory continued. "Luis informed me that Max caught you snooping through Senona's private magic books."

"I am terribly sorry, sir," Camille pleaded. "I just needed to know..."

"I know that you will never do that again," Luis replied sternly. "The next time I *will* have to tell my wife and you don't want to deal with her on those matters." Jeremy and Max nodded their heads vigorously.

Camille took a deep breath in relief.

"Despite her efforts to shield her thoughts, her plans became known to me in my night visions. As hard-headed as Camille is, I knew that if she didn't get to see her mother today then she would try again next year, or the next." Gregory laughed, "I am sure she gets that from me. So I asked my friends and Philip O'Sullivan to help me."

"Actually, I think she gets it from both sides of the family," Mercy corrected him.

"How did you know that we would go in the Asylum looking for Camille?" Jeremy asked.

"You are her closest friends and I knew. We knew," Gregory replied, looking at Luis and Anthony. "Each of you would help her, no matter what, as she would any of you. We didn't expect Max to be part of this, though."

"We almost didn't make it out," Ethan admitted. "Why did you wait to come and get us in the underworld rather than the Asylum?"

"Once the window of opportunity closes, no one can enter the Asylum," Gregory explained. "But we knew that once you came out into the underworld, Uncle Philip could take care of you."

"How did you know we were going to make it to the underworld?" Gretchen asked.

"We can't give away all our secrets," Anthony told his daughter. "Let's just say that we have lots of confidence in your abilities, and Philip has a friend named Mutt who kept a close eye on you for us."

"I believe you met him already. It helps

having friends in low places, too," Uncle Philip added with a wink and a chuckle.

Gregory explained how he had requested permission from Luis, Anthony and Atticus to allow this quest to be fulfilled. They all agreed that Camille would grow in her gifts, and provide some experience for the others, as well. Atticus had sent Mercy on a journey home which matched the time, and Gregory suspected she might have similar plans as Camille.

Mercy scowled at him, certain she was old enough to not need her father's supervision.

"We invited Philip O'Sullivan just in case we needed his kind of help," Gregory added, "and it is a good thing that we did!"

"One question sir," Ethan asked looking up at Camille's father.

"Ah yes, what about your mothers?" Gregory guessed. "As fathers, we decided to keep this one close to the chest. Your mothers, I am sure, are worried about where you have been for the past 4 hours."

"Only 4 hours?" Gretchen asked. "It seemed like 12 hours, at least."

"That is the underworld; the track of time does not flow straight there. Am I correct Philip?" Gregory asked.

"Well, that be why I am so young and good-looking still," Philip replied with a little jump and click of his heels, showing off his youthfulness.

Luis stared sternly at each of them. "I am pleased with your success and use of gifts throughout the Asylum. This remains our secret, however. If your mothers *ever* find out, the Time Chamber Asylum will be a walk in the park compared to what they will do to you."

"I know a little something that can seal those lips if it be too much for you," Uncle Philip offered. "Although the spilling of the secret may be something worth staying around to watch," he added thoughtfully.

"It's alright Uncle Philip; I know that we can keep this a secret," Jeremy replied quickly, thinking of what Uncle Philip might do to them if he thought too long.

Mercy was still holding on to Camille and Gregory. She said "I am so happy to be here with my family. I know that I speak for my sister as well when I say thank you, gentlemen, for helping us safely through this quest." She stepped forward and hugged Anthony and Luis.

"What about me?" Max asked, looking at

A. DRAGONBLOOD

Mercy. Everyone laughed as she gave Max a big hug, too.

"I have one big request for you, Camille!" Luis exclaimed heartily.

"Sure, whatever you want, sir!" Camille replied.

"Go out there on Monday and play some serious futbol. Bring that Southern Soccer Trophy home!"

"Over here!" A frantic cry broke the moment as Senona spotted them from across the square. She raced to them and half-hugged, half-spanked both her boys.

"We were just heading back to square," Gregory said calmly. "Look who we found on our way over here, hanging out with some art school students."

"Mercy, is that really you?" Helen peered behind Gregory, looking for Ethan. Mercy jumped towards her, dragging Ethan by the arm.

"Yes, Madame, it is me. I needed some southern love, and what better time to visit than St. Patrick's Day? I was planning to come over to the square shortly; I know where the real party is," Mercy replied nonchalantly.

Staring at Uncle Philip, Senona demanded,

"I am sure that you had something to do with them leaving the square!"

"Maybe, maybe not!" He was smiling as always. "Have you enjoyed those mints? You were certain that they were fools' candy, wasn't ya, Cailin?"

Senona ignored him. She turned and picked up Max. "Are you alright? Why did you leave too?"

Max smiled at her like Uncle Philip and told her that he wanted to be a big boy like Jeremy. Senona sighed deeply.

Frustrated and relieved, Helen said "You are all safe, that's what counts. It is St. Patrick's Day and we haven't made it down to River Street yet. But starting tomorrow you will have plenty of time to think about this. You are all grounded for leaving the square without telling anyone where you were going."

"That goes for all of you," Senona added.

Max smiled and replied "Cool!" since he had never been grounded before.

Jeremy, on the other hand, opened his mouth and then closed it. The others waited to see if Jeremy had anything to say, but this time he knew enough to keep his mouth shut. Mercy smiled at him and winked.

"I would ground you too Philip, if I could!"

Senona exclaimed. She turned to where she had last seen him, but he was gone. "That is just like him to leave when there is punishment being dealt out," she added in exasperation.

Gregory placed his arms around his daughters' shoulders and began walking towards River Street.

"Mommy told us something you may want to know about the Double M's," Camille whispered in his ear.

"Not today, my dear. We have some Irish partying to do," he replied.

Gregory announced, "I may not be Irish, but I have been known to spread a little blarney myself. First an Irish blessing:

"'May the light always find you on a dreary day,
When you need to be home, may you find your way,
May you always have courage to take a chance,
and never find frogs in your underpants.'"

All the children laughed and yelled, "'Erin Go Bragh!'"

START YOUR OWN STORY HERE.

On this page start your outline of a story that you would like to share with others. To find advice on writing visit my website.

_____

_____

_____

_____

_____

_____

_____

_____

_____

_____

_____

_____

_____

Read Ethan's Dragon story-
Simon and Vincent – The Dragon Mates

www.childrenoftheothers.com

FACTS ABOUT ST. PATRICK'S DAY

St. Patrick's Day is observed on March 17 because that is the feast day of St. Patrick, the patron saint of Ireland. It is believed that he died on March 17 in the year 461 AD and was born in 385A.D.

In Ireland on St. Patrick's Day, people traditionally wear a small bunch of shamrocks on their jackets or caps. Children wear orange, white and green badges, and women and girls wear green ribbons in their hair.

Many cities have a St. Patrick's Day parade. Dublin, the capital of Ireland, has a huge St. Patrick's Day festival from March 15-19 that features a parade, family carnivals, treasure hunts, dance, theatre and more. In North American, Chicago dyes the Chicago River green. There is a large St. Patrick's Day parade in Boston, Massachusetts and Savannah, Georgia. Montreal is home to Canada's longest running St. Patrick's Day parade.

FACTS ABOUT THE IRISH

34 million Americans have Irish ancestry, according to the 2003 US Census. That's almost nine times the population of Ireland, which has 4.1 million people.

The harp is the symbol of Ireland. The color green is also commonly associated with Ireland, also known as "the Emerald Isle."

The Irish flag is green, white and orange. The green symbolizes the people of the south, and orange is for the people of the north. White represents the peace that brings them together as a nation.

Legend says that each leaf of the clover means something: the first is for hope, the second for faith, the third for love and the fourth for luck.

I hope you enjoyed

Children of the Others
Collection™
Book III

SERENITY
FOR
ST. PATRICK'S DAY

Children of the Others
Collection™ Available Now

More Surprises, more danger,
more Children of The Others

<u>Fall 2011</u>

The story continues...

The Mirror Men are growing in numbers and it is up to Ethan, Camille, Jeremy, Gretchen, Mercy and the others to find out how and why they are controlling children. A summer vacation is just what they need to figure this out before no one is safe from the control of the Mirror Men.

The Children of the Others
Collection™

ABOUT THE AUTHOR

A. DRAGONBLOOD is a fiction writer who uses spell-binding flair, respect for diversity, humor, action, creative spookiness, imaginativeness and even everyday reality to create stories of plausible fantasy and ordinary magic for young readers.

TED KAY has been a professional artist for 15 years. Originally from Spartanburg SC, Ted found his home in the Savannah art scene 10 years ago. Savannah lends plenty of inspiration for his work with graphic novels, graphic design and illustrations.

CONTACT US @

On our interactive website Children of the Others. Leave a message, set up a school visit or contact your local book seller for a book signing.

www.childrenoftheothers.com

a.dragonblood@gmail.com